MY LOVE FOR YOU

THE SUMMER UNPLUGGED EPILOGUES BOOK 1

AMY SPARLING

AMY SPARLING

NOTE FROM THE AUTHOR

It all started with Summer Unplugged, which released in 2012. Now, eight years later, the series has 3 spin-offs and over 30 books.

This book takes place after the end of The Summer Unplugged series and before Jett's series, Believe in Me. If you'd like to read the entire series in order, here's a reading list:

- The Summer Unplugged Series
- The Summer Alone Series
- The Believe in Love Series
- The Summer Unplugged Epilogues (this book)

There are also 2 other series that take place in this same world with all new characters:

- The Love on the Track Series
- The Love at the Gym Series

Thank you for going on this journey with me and my characters!

ONE
BECCA

I've never really been around little kids. I had no siblings when I was growing up, and all my cousins are about my age or older. My best friend Bayleigh has a little brother, but we never hung out with him and certainly didn't spend time around him when he was a toddler. Maybe it's my lack of childcare knowledge that makes it such a surprise to discover that I love kids. Or maybe I just love Bayleigh's kid.

Jett Adams is the cutest three and a half year old you've ever seen. With a mop of curly dirty blond hair, he looks like a mini version of his dad, Jace Adams, and he has the heart of his mom. Many times when I see him he brings me a sweaty handful of flowers he's picked from around the yard. I think he learned that from his dad, who is always giving flowers to Bayleigh.

Jett is also ridiculously smart. I relax on the fold

out lounge chair in Bayleigh's backyard while I watch Jett ride his bicycle around. It's a kid's bike, powered by his feet on the pedals and not a motor or anything, but he pretends that it's a real dirt bike motorcycle like his dad's. Jett has a little dirt track in the back yard that Jace made for him with a tractor. It's a miniature little track with teensy dirt "jumps" that are basically just piles of dirt. As he pedals, he makes little motor sounds with his mouth, getting higher and louder as he "speeds up" on the long straight parts of the track. Then he lowers his voice during the turns. And here's what's really, really cute about this kid – he pretends to shift gears.

I know enough about motocross from watching Jace and my boyfriend, Park, to know that when their speedy dirt bikes come to a sharp turn, they downshift to slow down. The gear shift on the dirt bike makes a metallic *click-clunk* sound each time they do it. Jett knows this, too.

"Clu-clunk!" he says, pretending to shift imaginary gears on his bicycle. Then when he speeds up, he pedals really fast and makes a "weeeehhhh" throttle sound with his mouth, all while turning his right hand over the rubber handlebar grips, pretending it's a real dirt bike throttle.

This boy knows his way around a dirt bike and he's never even ridden a real one. I smile as I watch him. I cheer him on when he crosses the pretend finish line and throws his chubby little fists into the air.

"First place!" I call out. "Woohoo!"

He turns off the dirt path and pedals up to me. It's August, and the Texas heat is still going strong, and Jett is covered in sweat. I reach over to the wicker table next to me and hand him a sippy cup filled with ice water.

Jace and Bayleigh's house is really nice. It's also brand new since they recently had it constructed right here on their land. The back yard is vast and seems to stretch on forever out here in the Texas country. To the left is an actual dirt bike track, the business that Park and Jace own together. It's called: The Track. Boring name, but cool place. In the distance, you can hear the soft rumble of dirt bikes. It's no wonder little Jett loves dirt bikes so much. His dad is a former professional motocross racer, and his family owns a track.

Jett holds his sippy cup with both hands and gulps down the water. When he finishes, he puts the cup on the table and then he looks at me.

"What's wrong?" I ask.

He leans forward and cups his hands around his mouth. "I have to go potty," he whispers.

I chuckle, standing up as I reach for his hand. "Let's go to the bathroom, little dude."

Just a few years ago, I thought raising a kid would be hard. When Bayleigh got pregnant unexpectedly, she handled it so much better than I would have. I would have been a mess, constantly worried about what to do and how to take care of a little baby. Bayleigh was awesome at it, though. Of course, I'm sure it helps that she has such a great guy by her side. Jace is always there for her and Jett, and together they make an awesome little family.

Inside their house, I help Jett wash his hands and then I get a cool washcloth and wash off his face.

"Mommy will be home soon," I say as I clean him up. "You know what we should do before she gets here?"

"What?"

I turn toward the upturned bucket of toys in the living room. Jett wrinkles his face like cleaning up is the last thing he wants to do, but he walks over there anyway. Together we pick up all the toys and straighten the living room so that it looks nice and clean. I'm no child expert, but I like to think that every time I help teach Jett to clean up after himself, I'm embedding these habits into his personality. That way he'll grow up and be clean and tidy, unlike my own dad who still leaves all his crap all over the house and Mom constantly gripes at him for it.

Park is pretty clean, I guess. His house is a total mess right now because he bought an old Victorian home that is both huge and a fixer-upper. He's been remodeling it and living in it at the same time, so I guess I really have no idea if my boyfriend is clean or not. Since his house is always partly being remodeled, I guess he's done a pretty good job of keeping things as tidy as they can be.

My phone beeps with a text from Bayleigh.

Bay: Sorry this is taking so long! Traffic is a nightmare.

Me: No worries! We are having fun over here!

Today Bayleigh went to get her hair done at a real, official salon. It's been forever since she's done that. Being a mom has been her number one priority so she never wanted to take time for herself, but I finally convinced her that she deserves to treat herself every now and then. My best friend does so much for everyone else. She needs to do something for herself for once.

After everything is cleaned up, Jett begs me to go back outside with him. This time we play on the swing set. This swing set used to have those child-safe swings on them where you put the kid's legs through the holes, but a few months ago Jett went to a park and played on the real swings and decided he liked them better.

Jace replaced the child swings with normal ones, and now I'm terrified of hurting the kid.

"Higher!" he squeals as I push him on the swing.

I push a teensy bit harder. "Higher Aunt Becca!"

"That's as high as it goes," I say.

He shakes his head. "Nuh-uh! Daddy can go higher."

"Well Daddy is stronger than I am," I say.

The last thing I'd want is to push Jett so high that he falls off and gets hurt on my watch. This kid is a little dare devil. He has no fear at all, which I'm certain he's inherited from his dad, who is also a dare devil. These motocross guys fly through the air at crazy fast speeds and don't even think twice about it.

I glance across the yard and see a figure walking toward us from The Track. My heart warms and starts beating a little faster, just like it always does when I see Park. He's wearing his motocross riding pants and a tight-fitting white undershirt, which means he was out there riding his dirt bike instead of working. He likes to pretend the two are the same thing, but there is a big difference in riding around on a track having fun and sitting at his desk doing actual business work. Of course, when you're the boss, you can do whatever you want.

I wish he'd take off the undershirt, but the sight of him doing that little motocross swagger of his is still sexy. Just like Jett, Park's hair is a bit sweaty and disheveled. Boys and playing outside—guess it doesn't matter how old they get, they still love being outdoors.

"Hey, beautiful," Park says, pressing a kiss to my forehead.

"Park!" Jett calls out, twisting in his swing to see him. "Push me higher!"

"Okay!" he says.

I give him a look. "I don't want him to get hurt," I whisper.

"Aww, he's fine," Park says, giving him a hard push on the swing that sends him much higher than I was pushing. My heart skips a beat. The swing set only goes so high, but I still don't want this little toddler to fall. I rush around to the front of it while Park pushes him.

"Hold on tight," I tell Jett, who is all smiles.

"I am!" he calls out happily. "Park! I wanna jump!"

My eyes widen. Oh hell no. Park laughs and then gives Jett one hard push before walking around to the front of the swing set and standing in front of him.

"Are you kidding me?" I hiss.

Park grins. "We do this all the time." To Jett, he says, "Ready?"

Jett nods. I panic. Park holds out his arms. As soon as Jett swings forward, he lets go and launches himself out of the swing...

...right into Park's arms.

"Gotcha!" Park says, setting him down on the ground.

"Again!" Jett squeals, rushing back to the swing set.

I put a hand on my chest as if that will calm my racing heart. "I can't believe you did that!"

Park grins. "We do it all the time, babe."

"But he could have died!"

"Nah, I got him," Park assures me while Jett scrambles back on the swing and kicks his feet on the ground to get going again. "It's our thing."

"I don't like him jumping out of swings," I say. "I don't want him to get hurt on my watch."

"Okay, babe." Park's shoulders fall, then he nods. "You're the official babysitter, so you're the boss." To Jett he says, "Hey buddy, you wanna see my new dirt bike graphics?"

Jett's eyes widen and he jumps off the swing. Luckily it's not going high. "Yes!"

Park reaches out a hand and Jett grabs it. Together we walk toward The Track. It's a large dirt bike track that also has a building up front near the road. That's where the lobby and all the offices are, and just behind it is a garage area where the guys keep their dirt bikes since Park and Jett are both owners but also dirt bike riders.

We head to the garage. Park has two bikes and one of them just got all new stickers put on the gas tank and fenders. They've been customized with The Track logo and they look really good. Jett begs to sit on the bike, so Park lifts him up and sets him on the seat. It's a huge dirt bike—way bigger than anything I'd feel comfortable riding since my feet can't even touch the ground when I sit on it—but Jett looks at home and he's only three years old.

He stretches forward, his fingertips barely

reaching the handlebars and he's grinning widely as he makes little dirt bike sounds while sitting on this real dirt bike. Park stands next to him, keeping a protective arm out just in case Jett starts to fall. He looks over at me. "I love this kid."

"I love him, too," I say. He's my godson, and as far as I'm concerned, he's my real family too.

"Do you want kids?" Park asks me. I startle at the unexpected question. Park and I are in a serious relationship, but we're not married or anything.

"Yes," I say after a moment of thought. "I really do."

Park's lips split into a grin. "Me too."

TWO
PARK

I take a deep breath... and let it out slowly.

It does absolutely nothing to calm my nerves. Whoever invented deep breathing clearly never asked their girlfriend's parents for permission to marry their daughter. If they had, they'd know that no amount of breathing will make you any less nervous.

I chew on the inside of my lip, then try taking another breath even though I know it's pointless. Becca is at The Track working in the front lobby. She's the only person working today so I know she's stuck there and can't leave, which is good because I don't want her coming home to her parent's house and wondering why I'm here. This has to be a surprise.

And it has to go well.

What if they don't give me their blessing? What

if Becca's dad, the huge and intimidating cop, tells me hell no I'm not allowed to marry his daughter? A cold shudder of fear runs through me. I've met her dad a few times and things have always gone well. But this is different. Much different.

With a lump in my throat and a nervous system on overdrive, I get out of my truck and walk up to Becca's house. I ring the doorbell. Then I stand here and wait.

Mrs. Sosa opens the door. She smiles this wide, welcoming smile. "Hello, Park." She glances behind me, probably wondering if her daughter is with me, because there's no reason I should be coming over here alone. Becca only lives here half the time lately —the other half of the time she's crashing at my place. I want it to be *our* place. That's why I'm here.

"Hi, Mrs. Sosa," I say, surprised that my voice came out even and not filled with fear. "I hope you're not busy. I was wondering if I could have a word with you and Sergeant Sosa?"

"Of course," she says, stepping inside the house. "Come on in."

Becca's dad is tall and stout with tanned skin and lines in his forehead that are probably from years of arresting criminals. He's sitting in the living room watching TV when we walk in. My anxiety ramps up even more when he stands and greets me. I get visions of him throwing me in jail because he doesn't want me to marry his daughter.

"Hi, there," Mr. Sosa says, standing up and shaking my hand. "What's up?"

I clear my throat. Becca's parents stand next to each other, facing me.

"Mr. and Mrs. Sosa," I say, suddenly forgetting all the things I had practiced over the last few days. I've lied awake in bed rehearsing this moment, I've dreamt of this moment. I've even said it out loud in my truck while driving. I had an entire speech about how much I loved their daughter and now that I'm facing them, I've forgotten it all.

"I'd like to ask permission to marry your daughter."

There, I said it. They're still looking at me. Now they look at each other. A few seconds pass. And then they both smile.

Oh thank God.

I smile too, having suddenly found my voice. "Becca is the greatest thing that's ever happened to me. I love her more than I love anyone, or anything. I want to make her the happiest woman on earth. I will never, ever stop trying to be the best husband for her."

"Aww, sweetheart," Mrs. Sosa says. She pulls me into a hug.

But a hug is not exactly permission... I look at Mr. Sosa, who is staring at me with a contemplating look in his dark eyes. "Son," he says. Then he stares at me some more. Maybe only a few seconds pass.

Maybe an hour passes. I have no idea. I am so nervous. If he says no, my whole life will be ruined. I don't want to ask Becca to marry me without her father's blessing.

Mr. Sosa's lips press together.

Then they tip into a grin. "I'd be happy to have you as my son-in-law."

Relief washes over me. I swear I can hear angels singing.

"Thank you," I say. He reaches out and shakes my hand, then pulls me in for what is the manliest of manly hugs from the hardened old cop.

"When are you going to propose?" Mrs. Sosa asks me. Her eyes sparkle with anticipation.

I grin. "Soon."

I AM MUCH LESS nervous when I break the news to Jace. "I'm going to propose to Becca."

"It's about time," he says, smacking me on the shoulder. "You two have been dating forever."

"Just a couple of years," I say, rolling my eyes. "I wanted to wait until the right time."

When Becca and I first started dating, it was a little rocky. I lived in California and she lived here in Texas. Then when I moved here, Jace and Bayleigh were having their kid and we were starting the business, and it just didn't feel like the right time to try to get married in the middle of that. Plus, my biggest fear was that the business would fail and I'd run out of money and be a broke loser with no way to care for a wife of my own.

Luckily, the business is booming. I still have plenty of money saved from my professional racing days and my relationship with Becca is stronger than ever. Now is the perfect time to get married.

Once again, I'm sneaking around. When Becca and Bayleigh are working at The Track, Jace and I make up an excuse about needing to visit the company that maintains our tractors. It'll buy us a few hours of time to go shopping for rings.

We head into town and stop at this large jewelry store that's near the mall. It's a big brand name jeweler that has a million commercials on the radio and on TV. It's supposed to be the best place to buy an engagement ring. But I don't like anything they have. It's all too commercial and boring. Becca doesn't need a mass produced ring. She needs something special.

We drive to two more jewelry stores only to discover the same thing. The rings all look the same. They're all boring. None of the sparkling diamonds or shiny gold bands seem to fit Becca's personality. They're all just average. I need better than average.

"What did you buy Bayleigh?" I ask Jace as we sit in my truck, defeated, after visiting the third jewelry store in town.

"I had it custom ordered from a jeweler in SoCal," Jace says.

I nod. "Good call, man. Why didn't I think of that?"

He laughs. "Because I'm amazing at romance and you were a player for most of your life."

I roll my eyes. But I guess he's right.

We give up on ring searching and instead we head to a burger place in town to get some lunch. While we eat, I research jewelers online, trying to find the perfect place to custom order a ring.

"This is going to take forever," I say with a sigh. "I wanted to propose soon."

Jace shrugs and bites into his burger. "Forever is how long your marriage will last. Getting a ring is just a few weeks."

I know he's right. But that doesn't make me any less anxious. I've known Becca is the girl for me ever since I met her. I'm so ready to marry this woman and make her mine forever. But I guess I can wait a few weeks, especially if it means giving her a custom ring that no other woman in the world has.

"Here's a question since you're apparently Mr. Romantic," I say, looking at Jace.

"Hit me," he says.

"The proposal... how should I do it? Big and flashy with lots of people around, or small and quiet with just the two of us?"

Jace eats a French fry. "Man, I don't know."

"I thought you were Mr. Romantic."

He chuckles. "Yeah, yeah. Okay, so... does Becca seem like she'd want a big fancy proposal?"

I suck in air through my teeth. "Not really."

Becca is soft spoken and more reserved. That's one of the reasons I love her. She's not a wild and crazy fangirl like some motocross girls I've known in my life. She's sweet.

"I tell you what," Jace says over a mouthful of food. "You shouldn't be asking yourself big proposal or small proposal. You should ask yourself what fits Becca? What fits both of you? Is there some part of your relationship that is uniquely you guys? That's what you should use to make your proposal. Make it unique to her."

Chills prickle over my arms.

"You're a genius," I say as the perfect proposal idea comes to me.

"Duh." Jace snorts and takes another bite of his burger. "I am Mr. Romantic, after all."

THREE
BECCA

I basically have two jobs right now. My part time gig at The Track is slowly becoming full time, because I help out whenever I'm needed, but lately the business is growing so popular and getting so many clients that Park and Jace need me a lot more than usual. I know Park is overpaying me for my job, but I don't complain. After all, I couldn't make this much money working at C&C all day.

My other job is Becca's Inspirations. I started out making inspirational artwork and selling it online. Now I have my own website and social media pages with about ten thousand followers and dozens of custom artwork requests each week. It keeps me busy and I'm able to save up a lot of money because I don't technically have to pay rent. I live halfway at home with my parents and halfway at Park's.

He gave me a key a long time ago, so I come and go as I please, but we've never had "the talk" about me living here full time. It's kind of awkward... but I know we love each other so I just put it out of my mind. I'm doing laundry at my parent's house when Park texts me.

Park: Are you still at The Track? I can't find you.
Me: No, I'm doing laundry
Park: you know there's a washing machine at my house, right?

I roll my eyes. YES I do know that. I helped him pick out the washer and dryer at Best Buy when he moved in! But that doesn't mean I'm just going to invite myself to wash my clothes at his place. It's still *his* place, after all.

Me: I'm not going to wash my clothes at your place.
Park: well you should come over for dinner.
Me: okay, should I get us some take out?
Park: Nope. Just bring yourself

After my clothes are dry, I put them away and then head over to Park's house. Every time I make this drive, I wonder why we haven't moved in together yet, especially since Bayleigh is constantly telling me just to move in with him already. But I don't want to assume. I just want him to ask me. Maybe I'll find a way to hint around about it tonight.

When I pull up in Park's driveway, he's sitting on the porch waiting for me. His house is an ancient Victorian style house that's white with freshly painted black shutters. They're the kind of shutters that actually work and aren't just for decoration. There's also a wraparound porch in the front with a new swing. He stands up from the porch as I get out of my car.

"Hey, beautiful."

"You always say that," I mutter as I lean into his open arms for a hug.

"It's not my fault," he says. "You're always beautiful."

I roll my eyes. That's hardly the truth. Right now I'm in black leggings and a motocross T-shirt I stole from Park ages ago. It's baggy on me and is super soft and comfortable. Plus it has his name on the back of it from when he raced professionally for Kawasaki, which I think is cool. Park just sees it as a boring remnant of his past life.

Instead of trying to cook something, Park has ordered take out from or favorite Italian place. He's being all cute tonight because he set up the food on the patio table out back since it's a perfect autumn evening outside. I sit opposite of him at the small table and he lights two tall candles that I didn't even know he had.

"Look at you being all romantic," I say, grinning as he sits across from me.

"I was just thinking that we've never had a candlelit dinner under the stars, so I figured we should fix that."

I look up. It's only about seven o'clock, so it's fairly dark outside but not too dark yet. I can see the half-moon in the sky, but that's about it.

"Okay...well, we *know* the stars are there," Park says, looking up. "Even if we can't see them."

I laugh and dive into my food. When we're done eating, Park stands up and reaches for my hand. I take it and stand up next to him. His arms circle around my waist and we stand here under the invisible stars for a few moments. I lean up on my toes and kiss him.

"I have an idea," he says while his lips are still pressed to mine. He kisses me and then pulls back a bit to look into my eyes. "I was thinking you could teach me to paint."

"Oh yeah?" I say, lifting a brow. "You painted this whole house, what else is there to paint?"

"I mean artwork," he says. "You make me art all the time. I want to make you something."

I grin. "Okay, that could be fun. When?"

"Now?"

I take his hand and we walk upstairs. The house is technically just two full stories, but there's a third flight of stairs that lead up to a small room with large windows that overlook the property. This room is my painting studio. Park set it up for me when he first moved in. It's great because I don't have much room at my parent's house to paint. My bedroom has new carpet and all my things that I don't want to get dirty, and the garage is full of Dad's tools and years of junk so there's not much room there. This studio is the best.

I have to easels up here; my old one that's kind of crappy, and the new one Park bought me a while back. I let him use the new one. I set up a fresh new canvas for him. I open the windows to let in the cool breeze and also to let out the paint fumes. Park plays some music on the Bluetooth speaker in the middle of the room.

He sits on the stool in front of his easel. "Okay, Miss Art Teacher. What's first?"

"I start with a base color," I say, showing him my shelf of paint. I have every color you can get from the local art store. We pick our paints and I show him the different sized paint brushes, and which one works best for painting a background. Once we start paint-ing, Park turns his easel away from mine.

"My artwork is a secret," he says, grinning at me over the canvas. "You can't see it until it's done."

I roll my eyes. "I can't give you pointers if you don't let me see."

He shrugs. "That's okay. I'll wing it."

I decide to paint the night sky, using the real sky as my inspiration. I cover my canvas in black and then smooth layers of dark blue and lighter blue on top of it. I explain what I'm doing every step of the way so that Park has some idea of what he can do as well even if he is keeping his painting a secret from me.

We sing along to the music and tell each other about our day while we work. It's fun having him up here. I get an old brush and flick the bristles to splatter white paint drops all over my canvas, giving the impression of stars. It's really turning out well, but I'm not sure what quote I want to paint on top of it yet.

My signature style is to paint each canvas with an inspirational or motivational quote, but I can't think of any right now. Plus, this night sky is turning out so pretty, maybe it doesn't need a quote.

A short while later, Park peers at me over his canvas. "I'm done."

"Oh yeah?" I say, standing up. "Can I see it?"

His eyes drop to the painting and then look back up at me. "Yep."

He steps out of the way. I walk around to his side of the studio to see the canvas he's kept turned away from me this whole time. My jaw drops. My vision blurs.

At first I'm not even sure I'm reading it right. Maybe my mind is making up silly things it wants to see. But when I blink, it's right there in front of me.

Park has painted a sky as well, but his is made with oranges and pinks and has a sun setting on the horizon. Across the sky, painted in his handwriting are the words:

Will you marry me?

Everything goes still. I turn to look at him and he's on one knee. He holds a black velvety ring box in his hand. The paint studio lights make his eyes sparkle. Tears flood into mine.

"Becca, sweetheart. Will you marry me?"

Okay, now I'm seriously crying. I reach for a paintbrush and dip it into a bit of dark blue paint— the closest color next to me. While Park kneels in front of me I turn to his canvas and paint the word *yes*.

Park stands up and wraps me in a hug. I think we're both crying. When he pulls away, he slides the most beautiful ring I've ever seen onto my finger. I marvel at the sparkles. This ring seems to make the whole room glow. I'm so overwhelmed I don't know what to do. I want to admire my ring. I want to kiss him. I want to jump up and down and scream in happiness.

I reach up and take his scruffy face in my hands,

then I kiss him. My heart is fluttering, my knees are weak, and my lips tingle with warmth. I take a deep breath and close my eyes and we just hold each other, basking in this moment.

I think it might be the best moment I've ever experienced.

FOUR
PARK

I didn't realize how much work goes into getting married. It's not just about the proposal and the wedding day—it's so much more. Case in point: tonight is our "Engagement Party." I had no idea such a thing existed, but once we announced we became engaged, Bayleigh and Jace insisted on throwing us a party. Since all of our other friends and family members kept asking when the party would be, I guess this is a normal thing. There's also a bridal shower that Bayleigh is throwing for Becca, and then of course, the bachelor and bachelorette parties.

Getting married is all about partying, apparently. I just want to spend the rest of my life with Becca, but I'm happy to go along for the ride.

Tonight's engagement party is taking place at La Casona, a family-owned Mexican restaurant in town. They have a party room available behind the restau-

rant and Jace has rented it out. Bayleigh and Becca's
mom spent all day decorating. They also handled the
guest list and everything. Becca and I are just
supposed to show up at six o'clock and have fun.

When I get out of the shower, Becca is standing
in front of the large mirror above the dresser. Her
auburn hair is long and curled, and the room smells
like hair spray. She's wearing a pink dress that stops
just above her knees. She's also wearing two different
shoes.

"Nice shoes," I say with a chuckle.

She turns around to face me. "Which one looks
better?"

She holds out her left foot which has a black
sandal on it. Then she holds out the other foot,
which has a silver sandal.

I shrug. "They both look good."

She groans and turns back to the mirror. "Babe,
you are useless in the fashion department."

"I'm good in other departments," I say, walking
up behind her. All I'm wearing is a towel wrapped
around my waist. I grab her hips and pull her up
against me.

"Yes you are," she says, her voice a little breathy.
I watch her in the mirror in front of us, then I kiss her
neck. Chills rise up along her soft skin. With one last
squeeze of her hips, I let her go. If I let myself get
distracted, we'll be late to our own party.

I throw on the outfit Becca has chosen for me, a

black button up shirt and my tight jeans. If being married means I never have to worry about what to wear to parties, that's just one more benefit of proposing. You know, besides the benefit of spending my life with my soul mate.

When we arrive at the restaurant, we discover the party room isn't just a room. It's an entire building behind the main restaurant. There are lights and decorations and music. It's like a mini restaurant that you get all to yourselves for the night. The place is filled with all of our friends and Becca's family. When Bayleigh asked for my parents' information, I had told her I'd be happier without them traveling from California. I'm sure they would come if invited, but it's my party and I don't want to see them.

Becca and I sit at a table in the center of the room. Bayleigh puts a sash across our chests. Mine says Groom, and Becca's says Bride. I hardly get to talk to my bride, since everyone wants to come up and say hello and take pictures with us. Overall, it's still a great night.

The restaurant caters the event, so I get a huge plate of fajitas and sit next to Jace. There's also an unlimited self-serve margarita bar next to the food. Becca tries to eat, but she's caught up in so many conversations, she ends up standing in the middle of the room holding an empty plate for half an hour.

Jace slides into the empty chair next to me. "This food is pretty good."

"Yeah it is. We have to start coming here for dinner."

"For sure," he says, reaching for a tortilla chip. "You know your girl is drunk, right?"

"Huh?" I search across the room for Becca. When my eyes land on her, she's smiling, laughing it up with a group of girlfriends. The cup in her hand is empty, but she tries to take a sip from it anyway. I laugh. "I should probably go check on her."

I get up and saunter over to Becca, arriving just when someone says something funny. Or at least everyone thinks it's funny because all three girls burst out laughing. Becca's face lights up when she sees me. "Babe!"

"Hi," I say, putting an arm around her back

"Hi," she says back, giving me a cheesy, tipsy grin. "These margaritas are good."

She tips the cup to her lips but nothing comes out because it's empty. She frowns. "Boo."

"How drunk are you?" I ask. Becca doesn't exactly drink often. I'm not one to tell a woman what she can and can't do, but I also don't want her to get sick.

Her eyes widen in surprise. "Oh crap," she whispers. Or at least, she thinks she whispers it... she's actually whisper-yelling. Luckily the music is loud so no one cares or notices. "I *am* drunk!"

She collapses into giggles and tries to drink from her cup again.

I laugh. "You are the cutest drunk in the world."

"Psh..." she says, waving her hand at me. "I need another drink. Where are the drinks?"

"How about I get it for you?" I say.

She grins up at me, then lifts on her toes and kisses me. Her lips taste like lime. "You're the best."

As I walk over to the margarita machines, I can't help but smile. My life is absolutely perfect.

FIVE
BECCA

So much in my life is changing and it's all happening so quickly. At times I feel overwhelmed, but it's a good sort of overwhelm. I spend my days excited and I go to bed feeling giddy and eager for the next day. Today, I'm at my parent's house, packing up all my things. Yep. It's finally happening.

I'm moving in with Park.

Park is coming over here when he gets off work and we'll start loading up my stuff into his truck. I'm leaving my bedroom furniture because I won't need it at Park's house. Well... I guess it'll be my house too, soon enough. Park has a king sized bed and a huge dresser that only has two drawers filled with his stuff. The rest will be mine.

After the engagement party a few days ago, Park had taken me home back to his place and we fell asleep in bed together. I wasn't super drunk, but I was drunk enough to be all stupid and giggly like a complete dork. Park and I laid in his bed, cuddled up together, and I was slowly drifting off to sleep when he finally said the words I'd been wanting to hear forever.

"Will you move in with me?"

I told him I'd love to. And now here I am, hands on my hips as I stand in my room that I've lived in since I was a baby. I have so much stuff. I'm not even sure I want all of it.

I use big trash bags to throw all my clothes in, and then I put together some cardboard boxes for other items. I stand up on my bed and gently take down the clear lights that are strung up all over the place. I'm bringing the lights with me because I can hang them up in my paint studio.

I use this opportunity to make piles of things that I can donate because I'll never use them again. Then I go through my old school notebooks and journals and cringe at how awkward some of it is. I used to write about wishing I had a boyfriend. Now I have a fiancé. Crazy how life turns out.

I haul all the stuff I'm taking to Park's out to the living room and stack it neatly by the door. Mom walks in from the kitchen. Her eyes widen.

"You're leaving today?"

"Yeah..." I pull my sagging ponytail out and tie it back up tighter. "I told you this yesterday."

"I know, but... I thought it might take you a few days. This is all so sudden!"

She rushes over and wraps me in a hug. "You need some help?"

I shake my head. "I've got it. There's not much left. But I have some things I don't need to take with me so I might need to get a storage unit, or find room in Park's garage."

"Just leave it here," Mom says.

"You sure?"

"Of course." She waves her hand at me. "It's not like we need your room for anything else. Take as long as you need."

It's relieving to know my parents don't want me to get all my stuff out as soon as possible. I thought maybe they'd turn my room into some kind of guest room or man cave, or in Bayleigh's mom's case, a craft room.

Back in my childhood room, I look around at everything. My dresser drawers and closet are emptied. My bed is made, because I won't need the sheets since they are too small for Park's bed. There are a few pictures on my walls, but I don't really have a place for them at Park's house. Plus I want to add new pictures to his walls. I don't want to drag teenage photos over there—I want to make new memories.

Pretty soon we'll have engagement photos to hang on our walls. We've booked a photoshoot appointment with Clara Maize, who is one of the top photographers in Texas. She'll also photograph our wedding, and maybe one day, our baby photos.

I grin at the idea of taking baby photos with Park. I wonder what our kids will look like. If they have Park's genes, they'll be super cute.

My eyes land on the dry erase board on my wall. I put it up there a long time ago when I wanted to paint quotes on my walls and Mom wouldn't let me. I compromised by getting a white board so I could write whatever I wanted on it. I haven't updated it in a while. Right now it says:

Try to be a rainbow in someone else's cloud.

I love that phrase. I love that it's different from most inspirational quotes—it's not about making yourself happy or making yourself feel better. It's about making someone else feel better.

I smile and reach up, taking the white board off the wall. I'm not sure where it'll go in my new home, but it's coming with me. As I carry it out to the front door, I remember all the times I've written new quotes on this board over the years. I remember how these quotes are what inspired Becca's Inspirations, my own business that earns pretty good money for being a one-woman shop. Suddenly I'm thinking about Park and that summer we briefly met at C&C BMX Park when I first started working there. Then something strange occurs to me.

I call Bayleigh. When she answers I can hear

cartoons playing in the background. Such is the life of being the mom of a toddler, I suppose.

"What's up?" she says.

"I was just thinking... do you remember Ian?"

"Who?"

"Ian," I say, thinking back to a few years ago. "That guy you briefly dated in high school."

"Oh God. Ew. Ew, ew, ew," she says, making gagging sounds. "I can't believe I was so naive and stupid back then. Why would you call me to bring that up?"

I chuckle. "That's just it... Ian was a huge mistake in your life, but when you think about it... he kind of made both of our lives perfect. Because of Ian, you got grounded and sent to your grandparent's house and that's where you met Jace. And because you met Jace, I also met Park. Now we're living happily ever after, and it's all one hundred percent because of Ian."

"Wow." The cartoon music gets quieter in the background, so I'm guessing she walked out of the room. "I guess you're right."

"Weird, huh?" I say.

"Very, very, weird." She laughs. "I don't still talk to that loser but if I did, I'd send him a thank you card."

"We can just thank the Universe instead," I say. "She works in mysterious ways."

"That's for sure," Bayleigh says. "Thank you, Universe!"

Now I'm thinking of a new quote for my quote board. I'm not sure of the perfect words yet, but I want it to say something about how things find a way to work themselves out. About how even in the dark when all hope is lost, there's still something going on in the background. Something that could change everything for the better.

SIX
PARK

I stretch out my legs onto the huge ottoman thingy that goes with our couch. It's a large sectional that takes up most of the living room. Becca and I fell in love with it at the furniture store, even though we were there looking for barstools and not living room furniture. It got delivered today.

I lay back, stretching my arms out and wrapping one around Becca's shoulders. She's also stretched out on the big fluffy cushions, one leg on the couch, one on the floor.

"This is a really good couch."

"This is the best couch ever," she says. "I'm so glad we got it."

"I'm never leaving this spot. This spot is my forever home now."

Becca laughs. "I guess we'll just get married right here? Saves us time finding a venue."

I sink a little deeper into the couch, pulling Becca toward me. Her head rests on my chest while we watch TV. "Perfect."

She takes out her phone and opens the calendar. I'm mostly watching TV but I can't help but notice that she's spending a long time just scrolling through a calendar app.

"What ya doing?"

"I'm trying to find a good day for the wedding. What do you think?"

"How about tomorrow?" I say with a grin.

She rolls her eyes. "I want a wedding, not an elopement. You want one too, right?"

I nod. "Yeah. We could elope... but a wedding would be fun."

She sits up and turns to face me while still going through her phone. "I'm thinking a small wedding though... not big and crazy."

"Sounds good to me. I liked Jace's wedding. It was small."

She bites her lip. "I'm thinking maybe even smaller than that... like just very close friends and family. I don't really want a big fancy thing." She considers it a moment. "Well.. I want kind of fancy... but not big."

I laugh. "Whatever you want, I want too."

"So do we want a summer, spring, fall, or winter wedding?"

I snort. "We don't really have all four seasons in

Texas. It's either hot, or slightly less hot."

She gives my arm a playful shove. "It gets cold here! Just not winter wonderland cold."

"I don't care when we get married. I just want to get married."

She sighs. "That's romantic and all, but we still need to pick a date."

"Tomorrow," I say again.

She rolls her eyes.

"What about a Halloween wedding? That's next month."

"That's really early," Becca says as if she's actually considering a Halloween wedding when I was only joking. "Weddings take a long time to plan."

"Aw, but I wanted to dress up like Jack Skellington for our wedding," I say with a fake pout.

She pokes my stomach. "You are too thick to be Jack Skellington."

I put a hand on my stomach and make a face like my feelings are hurt. "This is muscle, not fat, for your information."

She laughs. "I know."

"So if I don't have the body for a Halloween wedding, maybe we should have a Thanksgiving wedding. I can just dress up like a big fat turkey."

"And we can have pumpkin pie instead of a wedding cake!" she jokes.

I shake my head. "No can do. I want a real cake. Pumpkin pie is gross."

"Okay, so Thanksgiving is off the table," she says, making a pretend X across the air as if she's crossing that day off the list of possible wedding dates. "The next holiday is Christmas. We can't get married on Christmas... that's just weird."

"Totally weird," I agree. "Then people would think they can give us one gift and have it count as a Christmas present and a wedding present. Not on my watch. I want two presents."

We laugh, and then Becca sits up straighter. "Seriously though... we'll need to pick a date eventually. I don't want to wait forever to get married. I just want to *be* married."

"Same," I say, reaching out and running my hand through her hair. "The next holiday after Christmas is New Years. Let's get married on the first day of the year."

I expect her to laugh it off like she did my other jokey suggestions. But she tilts her head and her lips slide to the corner of her mouth. "That's... kind of a great idea."

"Yeah?" I say.

She nods. "A New Year's wedding... we can start the rest of our lives together on the first day of a new year. It's romantic. And fun."

"I dig it."

She frowns. "But that would mean getting married at midnight... or the next day but New

Year's Day is when everyone is hungover from partying."

"Midnight, then."

"Will people come to a midnight wedding?"

"The people who love us will," I say confidently. I know Jace and Bayleigh won't think twice about it. Plus, it's already a holiday where most people are staying awake until midnight anyway.

"Oooh... we could have fireworks!" Her eyes seem to sparkle at the thought of it.

"That would be badass."

"So... are we doing this?" She looks at her calendar app again. "Are we getting married on January first?"

"I think so."

She grins, all toothy and excited. "Awesome. I'll add it to the calendar!" She adds the date, and I give her my phone so she can put it on my calendar too, then she falls against me, snuggling up against my chest.

It's the end of September, which means New Years is just three months away. A rush of adrenaline flows through me at the thought of it. In just three months, I'll be married. I'm already living with the love of my life, so I don't think much will change. It'll just be official.

I AM TOTALLY out of my element when it comes to planning a wedding. I guess I thought it would be as easy as attending my own engagement party. But unfortunately, no one plans your wedding for you. You have to make a million decisions, and as Becca and I soon find out, three months is basically an impossibly short time to plan a wedding. Everyone thinks we're crazy. People like the New Year's idea because it's fun and unique, but the fact that it's only three months away is the problem.

We look into dozens of local venues and they're all booked up. One place only makes reservations for a year in advance. They tell us we should wait until next New Year's Day to get married. Becca and I both agree that we want to be married now, not later.

I can tell it's wearing on my beautiful bride-to-be. She doesn't go up to her studio for several days, and instead spends her time in the front office at The Track, looking up wedding venues online. Jace and Bayleigh offer to let us get married at the same place they got married since they still own the property. It's a really nice gesture, but I can tell Becca wants to do her own thing, not just copy her best friend.

So we keep looking.

I'm busy at work training a new group of kids who want to be future motocross racers. It keeps me busy all day, but I use every spare moment I have to try to help out with the wedding planning. I talk to my students' parents and ask their opinions, hoping that one of these days someone will tell me the perfect idea. So far, everyone's ideas suck.

We live fairly close to the coast of Texas, so a beach wedding is possible. However, Texas is not known for their beaches. Compared to just about every other beach, the Texas coast is ugly. I don't want brown water and ugly sand to be the backdrop of the best day of our lives, so I nix the beach idea without even bringing it up to Becca.

On Friday, after a particularly slow day of work, I say goodbye to my last student and then I walk into the lobby, craving the blast of cold air from the air conditioning. It's the first week of October, but when you're outside in the sun covered head to toe in protective motocross gear, it's still hot.

Becca smiles at me without taking her eyes off the computer. "You look tired."

"I am," I say, walking up to her. I pull out the barstool next to her and sit down. "Remind me to give the next set of six year olds to Jett. Teaching teenagers is so much easier."

She chuckles. "But working with little kids will prepare you for when we have our own kids."

I shake my head. "Nope. Our own kids will be cool. These kids are annoying. One started crying because he wanted another juice box and didn't feel like riding anymore. I don't think he even wants a dirt bike but his dad is making him ride in the hopes that he'll become famous."

Her nose crinkles. "What a jerk."

"Any luck on finding a wedding venue?"

She lets out a defeated sigh. "Sadly, getting married on our couch is the best idea we've had."

I reach over rub her back. "Don't stress, babe. We'll figure it out."

The business phone rings and I reach over and hit the speakerphone button. Usually Becca answers it, but I'm trying to take some of her work load off since she's stressed about the wedding.

"You've reached The Track, this is Park. How can I help you?"

"Hi there," the voice on the other line says. It sounds like an older woman. "My name is Lucy Hill. I'm from the Treehouses at Greene. I just saw your website about motocross training and I wanted to see if it'd be a good fit for my grandson."

"Sure thing," I say. I talk with her about the training courses we offer. Here at The Track, we're a motocross track where you can come ride for fun, but Jace and I also offer our expertise as one-on-one training sessions, or in group classes like what I was doing today with the six year olds.

Lucy is very interested in setting up something for her thirteen year old grandson who has a dirt bike and loves racing, but isn't very good at it. I get her all set up with an introductory one-on-one lesson for next week. Beside me, Becca is searching "Texas wedding venues" on the computer.

Then I suddenly remember something this woman said. "Excuse me, but, I have a question," I tell the woman on the phone. "You said you're from a treehouse?"

She chuckles. "Yes, the Treehouses at Greene. It's a vacation spot my family and I run. We have beautiful luxury suites in the trees. Some are over fifty feet tall and they overlook the gorgeous Brazos River."

Becca looks over at me. I think we're thinking the same thing.

"Do you happen to host weddings there?"

"Oh yes, all the time. They have to be small weddings, though. We can only hold about fifty people on the property, but it's a gorgeous view."

"Do you have any openings on New Year's?"

"Let me check." The sound of a keyboard clacking fills the quiet air in the lobby of our building. I look over at Becca, who just Googled these treehouses. Lucy is right—they are beautiful. They're basically massive, luxurious hotel rooms that are in the trees. You get to each one by walking across long rope bridges and wooden split-log stairs. The website features photos of the weddings they've hosted. On the ground between the treehouses, they set up a small outdoor wedding that faces the river and a backdrop of trees and hills that make for a picturesque view. The best part is that Greene, Texas is only a couple hours away.

"As a matter of fact, I do have an opening," Lucy says. "Why? You wanna get married?"

I look at Becca. She nods eagerly.

"Yes, ma'am, I do," I say.

"You know that's only three months away?" Lucy asks.

"Yep."

She chuckles. "Okay then. Let's get you on the schedule!"

Three months. I'm getting married in three months!
Holy cow! Three months feels both really far away
and like no time at all. I can't believe we lucked into
finding that wedding venue, and not only that, it's
going to be free. Well, quid pro quo. Park and I
talked with Lucy for over an hour that day. She and
Park decided on a trade. He trains her grandson, and
she rents us the venue for free. In addition to the
reception area which is on the ground, there are
three separate treehouses. One is a perfect honey-
moon suite which Park and I will stay in the night
after we get married. The other two will be our bachelor and bachelorette rooms where we'll each get
ready for the wedding.

Our plan is to have a sort of all day party where
we hang out with our best friends and family until

nighttime, which is when we'll get married. If we time it right, we can say our vows just after midnight. It's all going to be so beautiful and perfect.

Now we just need to figure out the rest of the details.

Up first – my wedding dress.

On Saturday, I get my mom and my best friend together for a day of what will hopefully result in finding my perfect wedding dress. Bayleigh drives us in her new SUV, and my mom spends the whole drive into town talking about how she can't believe her little girl is "all grown up."

"It's really weird knowing that one day Jett will grow up and get married," Bayleigh says.

"Trust me, the time will fly," My mom says. "Jett will be all grown up before you know it."

I think about little Jett, who isn't even in kindergarten yet. It's hard to think that one day he'll be an adult, too. I also think about my future children and how badly I want to be a mom. But first, I need to get married, and getting married requires a dress.

We arrive at a large wedding dress store. This is where practically everyone gets their dress. Their website says they have over a thousand styles to choose from, but as soon as I walk in, I'm not so sure I even like the place.

The three of us are practically attacked by three eager sales ladies all at once. Once they discover that

I'm the bride, two of them seem disappointed that they won't be able to sell a dress to Mom or Bayleigh, and the third one pours all her energy into me. She acts like she's my best friend, putting her arm around me as we walk. I politely step out of her grip. She's asking me every single thing about myself, like it's any of her business.

"I just wanted to look around, if that's okay."

Her lips press into a thin smile. "Okay. Our store is arranged by the price of the dresses. So what's your budget? I'll let you know where to look."

I glance at my mom. When we talked about going dress shopping, she'd said she wanted to buy my dress for me. Park and I want to pay for the wedding ourselves, but my mom really wants to buy my dress. She told me she had a thousand dollars for it, and I told her there's no way I'm letting her spend that much.

"What do the dresses usually cost?" I ask Claudia, who is our sales lady.

"The average dress is around three to four thousand," she says. "You'll find those aisles over there. But our high end dresses can go for twenty or more."

My eyes almost pop out of my head with how surprised I am. "Three thousand dollars? I didn't want to spend more than a thousand!"

Claudia's enthusiasm wanes. I guess she gets paid commission based on how much money I spend.

She heaves a sigh. "Well, you'll find some budget dresses in the back of the store. The thousand dollar and below rack is back there. Let me know if you need any help!"

And then she's gone. Funny how people only care about you when they want to make money off you.

We venture to the "cheap" section of the store, even though I think a thousand dollars is nowhere near cheap. I try on a few dresses, and they're pretty but not spectacular.

Mom and Bayleigh fawn over me while I stand on a small circular podium in front of three large mirrors that show me the dress from all angles.

"This one is gorgeous," Bay says. I'm wearing a sleeveless white satin gown with some lace along the bodice. It is pretty. All the dresses I've tried on have been pretty. But none of them make me feel like I need to get married in them.

I turn and look at my reflection in the mirrors. Even my reflection seems sad. This was supposed to be fun, but it's really not.

"What do you think?" Mom says. "Which one did you like the best?"

There are six dresses draped over the back of the chair next to me. I've tried them all on, but I don't love any of them.

"None," I say.

Mom and Bayleigh look worried.

"Well, let's find some more!" Mom says, putting on her happy-go-lucky smile.

"Eh... I'd rather not. This place sucks."

Bayleigh stands up. "I feel you, girl. This place is like some snooty rich people store with way too many gowns to choose from. We'll find a better place."

I nod. "I agree. Let's go."

WE NEVER FIND A BETTER PLACE. Over the next two weekends, my mom and Bayleigh and I pile into the car and drive all over the place. I try on wedding dresses at seven stores and none of them are worthwhile. Luckily, the saleswomen at most of the other stores are nicer than the first one, but they're all just so—fake. They smile and laugh and tell me what they think I want to hear, which is that I look "absolutely beautiful" in every single dress. I know for a fact that I did not look like a mermaid in that one mermaid style dress I tried on.

I'm feeling so defeated. I'm ready to just get married in my pajamas for all I care. Park offers to go with me one day, but I don't want him to see my dress. I know it's a silly tradition, but I think it's a worthwhile tradition to make him wait until our wedding day to see me all dressed up.

Today, while on my lunch break from The Track, I drive to the dry cleaners to pick up my favorite winter coat. I get it dry cleaned every year so it's ready for when it gets cold outside. After I pick it up, I'm sitting in my car in the parking lot, texting Park to see if he wants me to get him some food while I'm out. That's when I notice the little shop next door to the dry cleaners.

Abigail's Gowns

It's a narrow storefront, with only a small glass window up front. The window features a mannequin that's wearing a stunning bright pink gown. It's like a mix between a prom dress and a wedding dress. I love it. I wonder if they have wedding dresses too? It can't hurt to look.

I get out and walk inside. The shop is narrow but long, and the whole place is filled with dresses. Way in the back is a wave of white satin and lace—the wedding gowns. Country music plays from the speakers and the whole place smells like vanilla. There is no one else around, so I just make my way toward the white dresses.

It's only two circular clothing racks, but there are several dresses hanging up in clear garment bags. They're all unique and different.

"Hello there."

The soft voice startles me. I turn around and notice the small shopkeeper. She's probably not even five feet tall, and maybe in her sixties, with long silver hair and a sweet smile.

"Hi," I say. "I'm looking for a wedding dress."

"You've found the right place," she says, giving me a warm smile. "These are all one hundred percent unique. I designed them myself."

"Wow," I say, eyes wide. "Did you sew them too?"

She nods. "Would you like to try some on?"

My face falls. I know what the mass produced gowns cost at the big wedding dress store. I can't even fathom what a handmade custom dress would cost.

"I don't think so," I say, chewing on my lip. "I'm not sure I can afford a handmade dress."

"I price them affordably," she says. "The simpler designs are around five hundred, but this one here," she says, reaching out to a sparkly gown, "It's the most expensive one at thirteen hundred. I hate charging so much but all those crystals are expensive."

"No way," I say, feeling some excitement for the first time since I started looking at wedding dresses. "My budget is a thousand dollars."

She smiles. "Looks like you've come to the right place."

While I try on these beautiful handmade gowns, I discover that this woman is Abigail herself. She's owned this shop since the 1980s and sewing is her passion. It's a small shop without much business, so the whole time I'm here, no one else comes in, and I have Abigail all to myself as I shop. She shares little behind-the-scenes details with me about each gown I try on. As I stand here on this podium in front of Abigail, wearing one of her creations, I find myself stuck in another problem entirely. I love all the dresses.

It'll be hard to pick just one.

"You said you'll be getting married at nighttime, right?" she asks.

"Yes, ma'am. Right at midnight."

She puts a finger to her lips. "I have the perfect gown..."

She disappears behind the second rack of gowns and then emerges with a garment bag, which she holds out to me. "When I designed this one I pictured it being worn at night."

I slip behind the silver curtain and carefully try on the dress. It's white satin with lace and rhinestones, but this one isn't sleeveless. It has mesh fabric sleeves that are nearly invisible on my arms, but the sleeves are decorated with tiny crystals that almost look like the night sky. The crystals also decorate the neckline. I know the moment I turn around and let Abigail tie up the bodice that this dress is the one.

It fits me perfectly.

"Wow," she says, spinning me around to look at the mirror. "You wouldn't even need alterations!"

"This is it," I breathe. I don't even look like myself in the mirror. I look... like a bride. "This is the one."

There's a jingle sound as the shop door opens. I'm standing on the small podium tucked away in the back corner, so I don't see who enters. Abigail does.

"Hello, Officer. How can I help you?"

"I saw my daughter's car out front. I thought she might be in here. I was just going to stop in and say hello."

"Dad?" I call out, leaning forward to see him over a rack of dresses. He's standing there in uniform.

"Becca?"

He walks through the store, his lumbering form and big bulky uniform seeming totally out of place around all these delicate dresses. He stops in front of me, his mouth slightly open. "Oh my God. You're beautiful."

"I think I just found my dress," I say, unable to stop smiling. "You're the first person to know about it."

Dad's smile turns all sappy. Small creases form in the corner of his eyes. "You look just like your mom."

An overwhelming sense of calm falls over me. Planning a wedding is stressful and doing it in three months is kind of crazy. But this dress—this dress is perfect.

"Have you bought it yet?" Dad asks.

"Not yet, but I am."

He reaches into his pocket and takes out his wallet, then he turns to Abigail. "This dress is on me."

EIGHT

PARK

So it turns out that only *some* little kids are annoying. Some are actually pretty cool. I had another junior training class this week with a bunch of five and six year olds and I was dreading it like crazy before we started. The last group of kids I trained were exhausting, annoying, crybabies. But these three kids were cool. They were eager to learn, and being so young, they were fearless. You have to be a degree of fearless to race motocross. Fear will only hold you back from doing what it takes to win.

After today's class, all three of the kids made huge improvements. I'm pumped. I'm feeling like I'm actually good at this whole teaching motocross thing. Once I say bye to their parents, I head to the garage and take out my bike. I haven't ridden in days. It's weird growing up and working a real job instead of getting paid to race dirt bikes. I miss my bike. I miss racing. But I don't ever regret quitting that job. I did it so that I could be with Becca full time, and she's worth the sacrifice.

I crank up my bike and head to the track, pinning the throttle to feel the thrill of adrenaline as I soar across the dirt track. There's no greater rush than hitting a huge jump and flying through the air for those few seconds before you land. When Becca and I have kids, I hope they want to ride dirt bikes. Unlike some of the parents I come across at work, I won't force my kids into a sport they don't like. But with any luck, my kids will be little motocross stars.

I ride hard for about half an hour, and once my muscles are sore and my helmet feels covered in sweat, I decide to call it a day. Some people don't realize how much exercise riding a dirt bike actually is. It's not just sitting on a motorized bike. I stand the whole time, maneuvering the bike with my arms and legs. Motocross is a full body workout.

Back in the garage, I grab a clean towel and rub it over my head. It dries up the sweat, but I'm sure I smell like exhaust, dirt, and sweat. Ah well, Becca is used to it.

Inside the lobby, Becca and Bayleigh are hanging out at the front desk. They're both on their laptops with a big open binder between them. It's not just any binder—it's the wedding planning binder.

"What's up, ladies?" I say as I walk in. The lobby is air conditioned and feels great.

"Becca doesn't want a black and silver wedding," Bayleigh says without looking up from her computer screen. "What do you think?"

"Black and silver for a wedding?" I say, cocking an eyebrow.

"It's the classic New Year's Eve colors," she explains. Her hair is tied into a big ball of a bun on top of her head.

"Ah," I say, nodding in recognition. I've been to enough NYE parties to remember that now. "That would be kind of cool."

"No," Becca says. Her face squishes up in disapproval. "There's just something about it I don't like... I know we're doing NYE and everything but I don't like black and silver."

I walk up behind her and kiss the top of her head and then take a couple steps back so she doesn't have to smell me. Her computer screen is open to an online image search of black and silver party decorations. She's right. They don't look that good.

"What other colors are you considering?" I ask.

She looks at Bayleigh and they laugh. Clearly I'm missing out on some kind of joke. Becca shrugs. "I have no idea."

"There's only so many colors," I say, trying to be helpful. "What about blue?"

"Blue and?" she says.

"Huh?"

"We need two or three colors to have a real color theme."

"And they have to coordinate," Bayleigh says. She taps a page on the binder. She's printed out some kind of wedding planning list, which says to choose two to three coordinating colors for your wedding.

I roll my eyes. "Okay... blue and silver. Or blue and white. Dark blue, like the night sky and stars."

The two women look at each other for a long moment. I guess they've been best friends so long they can communicate without talking. A few seconds later, Becca grins. "Okay... I like it..."

"Me too," Bayleigh says. "Shall we Google?"

Becca wiggles her eyebrows. "We shall."

They both turn to their laptops and search the color scheme, which brings up tons of photos. It only took me two seconds to think of those colors, but a night sky theme would look really good. All the online inspiration photos in those colors are gorgeous. I'm not even someone who cares about that stuff normally, but even I know it's a good color theme.

Becca excitedly sucks in air through her teeth. "This is perfect! Do you know how long we've been working on colors? Like all freaking day."

I laugh, putting a hand to my chest. "Should have called me earlier. I'm a pro."

"Okay, then Mister Professional Wedding Planner," she says, sliding off the stool and standing in front of me. "If you're so smart, what kind of meal are we going to serve at the reception?"

"Uh..." I look up, trying to think of something. But I have no idea. Weddings usually have boring food at them, at least they did at the few weddings I've been to. "Delicious food," I say.

She slides her hands up my chest, peering up at me. "But what kind of delicious food?"

"Umm..."

She laughs. "Looks like you've ran out of good ideas for the day."

I sigh. "Sorry, ladies."

"That's okay," Bayleigh says. She's been furiously typing on her computer and writing in the planning binder. "You solved our color theme crisis, so this is still a pretty good day."

"Anything else I can help with?" I ask. I'm dying to get home and shower but I also feel some sense of obligation. It's my own wedding, after all. I feel like I should be helping more.

Becca shakes her head. "We can pick music over dinner tonight. You should go home and shower."

This woman is perfect. She's also a mind reader.

"Awesome," I say, giving her a quick kiss. "You're the best."

She smiles. "I know."

NINE

BECCA

The dollar store has so many great Halloween decorations, and the best part is they're cheap! I decide to take a day off from all the chaotic wedding planning and decorate our house and The Track to get in the holiday spirit. Decorating is much more fun than stressing over wedding planning. I know all the planning still needs to happen, but I'm trying to make my own wedding into something fun. Hence the day off.

I'm standing on a short stepladder hanging black and orange Halloween garland from the ceiling when the door opens and Jett comes rushing in.

"Aunt Becca!" he calls out, "I'm Batman!"

And he certainly is. He's wearing the classic Batman face mask and a batman body suit that's stuffed with fake muscles. It's freaking adorable.

"Wow, you look so cool!" I say.

Bayleigh comes in a few seconds later. Jett likes to run everywhere he goes, so he's always the first one in. My best friend, however, prefers to walk.

"Ooh, decorations!" Bayleigh says as she takes in the four bags on the floor that are filled with dollar store stuff. "Need some help?"

"Sure," I say.

"Hey Batman," she says to her son. "You want to go watch a movie?"

He nods and runs down the hall. We've set up one of the offices as a playroom for Jett, and there's a video monitor in there so we can keep an eye on him while we're up front. After she sets him up with a movie to watch, Bayleigh joins in on the decorations.

I may have gone a little overboard with the decorations, but I don't care. It's fun hanging up tons of garlands and streamers and stretching those fake spiderwebs all over the place. I found several strands of purple lights, which I tape around the front desk to give it a creepy glow.

"I really wanted to make Jett's costume this year," Bayleigh says. The roll of tape is in her mouth while she works, so her words are mumbled. "But he insisted on Batman and there's just no way I can make that costume with fabric and hot glue."

I laugh. "Luckily he's still young so you can make his costumes for years to come."

"I can't wait until you have a kid," she says, pulling off another piece of tape and pressing it to hold a plastic ghost into place on the wall. "We can dress the kids up in matching costumes!"

"Are you glad that Jett's a boy?" I ask as I mull over the idea of my future kids. "Or would you rather have had a girl?"

She shrugs. "I think I'd love either one just the same. I want another kid someday... but not now." She tosses a small plastic pumpkin at me. "Now it's your turn."

I snort out a laugh. We like to imagine that one day we'll both have kids and they'll be best friends. Sometimes we joke that I'll have a girl and she and Jett will get married one day. Of course Jett's almost four years old now, and I won't have a baby for at least a year, or maybe longer. The farther apart they are in age, the less likely we'll have kids who grow up and date each other. It's kind of a silly thing to imagine, now that I think about it.

"I just need to get married first," I say as I open another package of decorations. "That seems like a hard enough task already. I don't even want to think about having a kid right now. I don't know how I would manage it."

"You could always get pregnant accidentally," Bayleigh says sarcastically. "It's worked out for me."

"I think you're like the only person from high school who got pregnant and actually like your life now," I say. She wasn't the only teen mom in our hometown, but she's the only one who is happy. I don't think that's random, either. Bayleigh met her soul mate when she met Jace. Those two were meant to be from day one. I know they're going to last forever. An unexpected baby could never change that.

"My life is pretty great," Bayleigh says, more to herself. "I don't think I stop to appreciate that as much as I should. It's so easy to get hung up on drama, especially in the motocross world."

"That's for sure," I say. When I first started dating Park, it was definitely a learning curve to accept that he was a popular motocross racer. Girls everywhere wanted him, and because of that, they hated me. It's weird being hated by people who don't even know you. It's even weirder trying to accept that your boyfriend wants *you*, and not the hundreds of girls all vying for his attention.

"Okay, so back to the baby talk," Bay says, giving me a mischievous grin. "Do you have any names picked out?"

"Oh gosh," I say with a big, sarcastic sigh. "I told you I can't even *think* about kids right now!"

She laughs and walks over to the counter where the baby monitor is. Jett is laying on a bean bag watching TV, safe and sound. "I just can't wait until you're up to your knees in dirty diapers every day. It'll be fun being moms together."

"Yes, it will be," I say, watching Jett on the screen. He's the sweetest little kid ever. I hope my kids are just like him. "How many more kids do you want?" I ask.

"Just like... one," Bayleigh says. "Maybe a girl this time?"

"What would you name her?"

"Brooke," she says so quickly it's obvious she's thought about it before.

I grin. "Maybe we'll get pregnant at the same time."

Bayleigh smiles wide. "Now that would be the ultimate best friend thing to do!"

The employee's only door opens down the hallway and Park walks in quickly. "I need a pen," he says, more to himself than to me as he goes straight for the drawer with the office supplies. He digs around and gets a pen and a small notebook of paper. When he looks up, he flinches. "Whoa... this place is a Halloween wonderland."

"Is it too much?" I ask, looking around. Bayleigh and I have definitely gone a bit overboard with the cute decorations.

"Nah," he says, his expression softening into a smile. "It looks cool. The kids will love it."

"Speaking of kids," Bayleigh says. "We were just talking about your future offspring. How many kids do you want?"

Park glances at me. "Tons."

My eyes widen. He laughs. "I don't know... how many kids do you want, babe?"

I shrug. "Two?"

"Or three," he says, wiggling his eyebrows at me.

"Why three?" Bayleigh asks.

"For one, we have a huge house," he says. "And also, statistically the more kids we have, the more likely one of them will become a dirt bike racer."

Bayleigh and I both roll our eyes.

"What?" Park says defensively. "A guy can dream! Jace already has Jett to be his protégée. I need one too."

"Over my dead body will my son ride dirt bikes," Bayleigh says, putting her hands on her hips.

Park and I both give her a look that says we don't believe that for one second.

"Really?" I say.

Dirt bikes are Jace's entire personality. Seems odd that they wouldn't let their kid also ride one since Jace and Bayleigh's life revolves around the sport and so does their livelihood.

Bayleigh sighs, then tosses her arms up. "I don't want him to ride, but he probably will. He's obsessed with Daddy, after all."

"Aww, he'll be fine," Park says reassuringly. "He'll have the best teacher on earth. And by that, I mean, me. Not Jace."

Bayleigh laughs. "I won't tell him you said that."

"Good. Because he'd kick my ass."

TEN

PARK

I stare at myself in the mirror, turning to the left and then the right. I bare my teeth like a wolf. Okay, well, maybe that doesn't work—I just look stupid and not wolfish. I take a step back and flex, watching my muscles tighten in my reflection. Nice.

I look like a damn good Jacob Black.

This long black wig actually fits pretty well and covers up all of my hair. I found the circular arm tattoo as a temporary tattoo online and placed it exactly where Jacob's tattoo is in the Twilight movies. For my costume, I'm just wearing an old pair of jeans that I cut off at the knees and frayed around the edges. I should probably get a better tan to look exactly like Taylor Lautner, the actor who plays Jacob, but it's too late for that now.

Becca is going to freak. She and Bayleigh often get into friendly Twilight arguments about which hunk in the best hunk. Becca is Team Jacob, and Bayleigh is Team Edward. We're having a little Halloween party tonight at The Track and Jace and I are going to surprise our ladies by dressing up as their favorite Twilight guy.

Since Halloween falls on a Saturday this year, we decided to open up all night for a spooky ride session. It's not exactly spooky—we didn't want to scare anyone and have them get hurt—so we just put up crime scene tape around the sides of the track, and some spiderwebs and big plastic spiders around the grass.

A few food trucks are going to show up tonight and we'll be playing classic Halloween movies on a large projector screen outside. Becca and Bayleigh will be handing out candy to all the kids who come by. It should be a fun time. This is one of those awesome things about being your own boss. If Jace and I want to have a Halloween party, we can.

My phone beeps. It's a photo message from Jace. I click on it and burst out laughing.

He's styled his hair into the classic Edward poufy hair and also sprayed it dark brown with temporary hair dye. He's wearing a gray button up shirt and dark skinny jeans, but the absolute best part ever is his face.

He put on makeup.

Just call me the makeup king, his text reads.

Jace's entire face is covered in white makeup and

then he dusted some glitter all over himself. It's freaking hilarious. I am suddenly extremely grateful that my girl's favorite character is the shirtless were-wolf and not the sparkly vampire.

The girls are going to freak, I text back.

Jace: Ready to go surprise them?
Me: Yeah, meet you in 5 mins

When Jace and I came up with the idea to dress like these guys for Halloween, we decided to make it a surprise for the girls. Becca and Bayleigh decided to dress up as characters from Jett's favorite books. Bayleigh is going to be Waldo from the *Where's Waldo* books and Becca is going as the mouse from *If You Give a Mouse A Cookie*. She found a big pillow that's shaped like a cookie that she'll carry around all night. Little Jett is going to be Batman.

If tonight were a competition, I know Jace and I would win.

I hop on my four wheeler and drive over to Jett's house. I'm wearing a black hoodie with the hood up to cover my hair just in case Becca were to look outside. Right now she and Bayleigh are in the front office of The Track, giving out candy. With any luck, they won't see us until we walk inside.

Jace looks even more hilarious in person. When he walks out to meet me, he purses his lips together.

"What are you doing?"

He does it again, tipping his head down. "I'm modeling," he says, pressing his lips together again. He turns to face the other direction. "I'm a broody vampire."

I bust out laughing. Seeing my best friend covered in glitter is the most hilarious thing ever.

I rev the throttle. "Get on, you broody vampire."

Jace climbs on behind me and I drive us to The Track, which is just across the field. Cars are already filling the parking lot and the sound of dirt bikes roar through the air. Looks like our little Halloween shindig is having a pretty good turn out so far. Who knew free candy would bring so much business?

Since it's a cool evening, the doors to the front office are propped open so kids and their elaborate costumes can come and go easily. When Jace and I walk up, Becca and Bayleigh's jaws drop.

"Where's Bella?" I say in a breathy voice, my eyes searching until they land on Becca. "There she is." I walk over and put my arm around her. "Baby, I'm the only werewolf for you."

"That's not Bella, this is Bella," Jace says, going up to Bayleigh. He makes his goofy broody face. "And she loves *me*, not you."

"You want to fight, old man?" I say, flexing my muscles. "Cause I'll transform into a wolf right now and rip your stony ass to pieces."

"I'd like to see you try," Jace says, baring his teeth. At some point on the four wheeler ride over here, he'd inserted those plastic vampire teeth in his mouth. It takes everything I have not to laugh. "Get out of here, dog," he says, giving me a look of contempt. "I can't stand the smell of you."

"At least I don't smell like a bloodsucker."

We are getting way too into this.

Becca and Bayleigh start laughing. Someone takes a picture of us from across the room. Another guy I recognize as one of our regular riders starts clapping. "Bravo," he says.

Becca's laughing so hard she has tears sliding down her cheeks and over the black whiskers she's drawn on with makeup. She's wearing a brown T-shirt and brown leggings with mouse ears and a fake tail that sticks out from the pair of overalls she found at the thrift store to complete her outfit.

"I love you so much," she says, putting a hand on my bare chest. "You have the tattoo and everything."

"What about my hair?" I say, brushing the silky fake strands over my shoulder. "Am I the sexiest werewolf you've ever seen?"

"Yes," she says, still laughing. "This is amazing."

"Where did you get all that glitter?" Bayleigh asks Jace.

"Glitter?" He cocks an eyebrow. "This is my real body. Unlike Park, I actually went out and became a vampire for you, my love."

Now I'm laughing. Our costumes are a huge hit. Everyone who comes in wants to get a photo of us—

especially the women and the moms of all the kids. Jace and I are happy to oblige because all these photos posted to social media will only increase people's awareness of our business. Plus, this is the first event like this where we've invited the community to come hang out, not just dirt bike people. Maybe we can do more things like this in the future to bring more business. All the financial gurus say small businesses are most likely to fail in their first few years. I refuse to fail. We are going to succeed.

It's well past midnight when the party finally winds down and we go home. Becca tosses her cookie pillow on the couch and lets out a sigh. "That was so much fun," she says, removing her headband mouse ears. "We should have a party at The Track for every holiday."

"I was thinking the same thing." I reach up to pull off my wig but she grabs my hand.

"Don't," she says, peering up at me. "Leave it on."

"Why?" I ask, but a split second later I see the desire in her gaze. "Ah..."

I slide my arms around her waist. "Are you looking at me that way because you think I look good with long hair or because you think Jacob looks good with long hair?"

She grins. "Maybe a little bit of both."

"Oh, Bella," I say, trying my best at a husky Taylor Lautner voice. "Your fiancé would be very upset if he knew you were lusting after another man."

She slides her fingers up my bare chest. "I don't have a fiancé. I'm Bella, not Becca, remember?"

I grin and kiss her. Her hands wrap tightly around my neck and she lifts up on her goes. I grab her butt and lift her off the floor. Her legs wrap around me and I walk her to the bedroom.

"You know what would be even sexier?" I whisper against her neck as I kiss her soft skin.

"What?" she says, her eyes closing as little goose-bumps rise along her arms.

In my seductive whisper, I say, "If you weren't dressed like a mouse."

She bursts out laughing, tossing her head back, then covering her face with her hands. "Oh my God," she says, giggling. "I'm totally ruining the mood with these overalls!"

I lay beside her on the bed. "Nah... it's not a mood killer at all. Because all I have to do is this..." I reach up and unhook the clasp on her shoulder strap.

"I like where this is going," Becca says, giving me that flirty look of hers that makes my heart stop.

"Good," I say, unhooking the other shoulder strap. "Because you're all the candy I need this Halloween."

ELEVEN
BECCA

As much as I loved the gaudy overly decorated lobby at work, I think I'll tone it down a bit when I decorate our house for fall. I love the orange and red decorations, the twine and little scarecrows, and glittery pumpkins, but there's something about Thanksgiving as a holiday that's not nearly as much fun as Halloween. That's a little ironic because Thanksgiving has the best food. It's because of the food that I might like Thanksgiving better than any other holiday.

I'm all alone as I push my small shopping cart through the aisles at our local hobby and home décor store. Bayleigh is exhausted and didn't have the energy to come with me, and my mom is busy visiting my grandparents to make sure they don't get screwed over with the new car they want to purchase. Park is at work, and I am bored, so I came here to shop.

I've only lived in our house less than two months so there's still quite a bit of work to do to turn the place into the home I want to have. For starters, Park is not a home decorating kind of person. He bought only the bare minimum furniture when he first moved in. Now that I'm here, we've been to the furniture store half a dozen times to get more stuff we needed. Like a full living room furniture set with a coffee table and end tables. (Park was using an upside town laundry basket as a coffee table when I moved in.) We got bedroom furniture and a new kitchen table and barstools to go under the granite bar. The idea of putting barstools there had never crossed his mind, despite the fact that he's the one who remodeled the kitchen to include the bar. I love this man, but he's terrible at home décor.

Which is why I'm here.

I peruse the aisles and find a fall themed table runner and a cute pumpkin and sunflower center-piece. I get a wreath for the front door and a cute welcome mat that says "Happy fall y'all" in this perfectly Texan way. When my cart is full and I'm a little scared to see how much money I'm spending, I decide it's time to get out of here before I do some real damage to my savings account.

At home, I unload all my new stuff, pulling off the tags and wrapping and finding new places for them around the house. This is so much more fun than wedding planning! The only person I have to worry about is myself. Well, and possibly Park, but I doubt he'll care what kind of holiday decorations I use. When it comes to the wedding, I need to think about our guests, and the location, and the future—will our wedding look dated and ugly in 15 years? Hopefully not, because those photos will be preserved forever.

But fall decorations... I can throw those away in a few years and get news ones.

I chuckle to myself as I stretch out a sunflower garland across the mantle over the fireplace. In all honesty, the wedding planning hasn't been too hard. I started watching those reality TV shows about weddings and bridezillas, and my wedding is nothing like those. I want it to be an amazing night, but I'm also pretty laid back about things, especially when I compare myself to reality TV drama queens.

I bought two of the fall welcome mats, so after I finish decorating the house, I walk the second one over to The Track. I slip into the back employee entrance. Jett sees me from the kid room and waves. I wave back.

The office area part of this building has a long, narrow hallway that leads up to the front lobby. It's right when I'm walking down the hall that I hear a woman's voice that stops me in my tracks.

"Who are you?" the voice says. I don't know why,

but something about the shrill, almost sarcastic tone of voice rubs me the wrong way. "You look much older than the person I'm looking for."

Huh? That's rude.

We have our part time employee Maria working the front desk today. Her son takes lessons with Park, and instead of paying for them, she works for us two days a week. She's in her late thirties, so she's not exactly old.

"I'm Maria," I hear her say. "How can I help you? Are you looking for someone in particular?"

"Yeah," the voice says with a snort. I walk a little further down the hallway. The woman comes into view. She's about my age... maybe a bit older. Her hair is long and wavy and has been died the blondest blonde available. She's wearing Nike shorts and running shoes that show off her tanned, toned legs. Up top, she's wearing a white tank with just enough room to show off her glorious boobs. I am instantly envious of how pretty this woman is, and I don't even know her.

She puts a hand on her hip. Her focus is entirely on Maria and she doesn't see me step into the room. "I'm looking for the girl who stole my man."

"Umm," Maria says, clearly uncomfortable as she fidgets with the pen in her hand. "There's not anyone around here... I don't know who you're talking about."

"Hello," I say in my overly polite customer

service voice. I walk up next to Maria behind the front counter. I am very much aware that I'm wearing a baggy Kawasaki T-shirt and a boring pair of shorts with black flip flops. My hair is pulled into a lazy ponytail and I'm not wearing any makeup because I'm lazy and have no one to impress.

To put it simply, this woman is a super model and I'm a crumpled up piece of garbage someone left in a back alley somewhere.

Still, I smile brightly at her. "How can I help you? Are you here to ride a dirt bike because that's pretty much all there is to do here."

Her eyes are green and framed with too-long eyelashes that must be fake. She stares at me, assessing me. As much as I'd like to shrink down and hide, I have seen this look on tons of women over the years. It's jealousy. It's catty. It's basically everything that decent women everywhere hate in other women.

"I'm visiting from Tennessee," she says, flashing me a smile that's somehow even brighter than mine. She must practice more than I do. "I thought I'd stop by and see the woman who stole Park from me and look her in the eyes."

I lift up my hands and then drop them. "Here I am. But you're clearly confused because I've stolen nothing."

She smirks. We're exactly the same height, but

she's somehow trying to peer down at me. It kind of works. Wow.

"So you're the new girlfriend?" Her eyes travel down me. "Wow..."

"No, actually, I'm not," I say.

My denial catches this bitch off guard because she flinches, her eyes widening. "You're not Becca? I'm here to see this Becca woman the internet is all going on about. Where is she? I need to see who stole my man."

"How was he your man?" I ask, tilting my head. My heart is pounding, but I refuse to let her see any sign of weakness in me.

"We were dating," she says, standing tall. "He was a player, for sure, but he wanted me more than anyone else. I know he would have settled down with me but then he met this random Texas girl and she must have blackmailed him or something because he would never have quit motocross for someone like her."

"You seem to know a lot about her for not even knowing what she looks like," I say.

A long time ago, her words may have bothered me. May have struck a chord and reared up a ton of jealousy in my heart. But things are different now. I know Park. I know him inside and out. I know his ex-girlfriends and I know there are no girls in Tennessee that he cared about. When he says that I'm the only girlfriend he's ever wanted to settle down with, I believe him.

"I heard rumors," she says, unaffected by my comment. "I heard she works here and I just wanted to see her."

"Why?" I say. "Starting drama for no reason? Why can't you just get over the fact that he clearly didn't like you as much as you liked him?"

She scoffs. "Oh, he did. He was basically obsessed with me. Now will you please find me his girlfriend?"

"I'm afraid I can't do that," I say. Beside me, Maria is still as a board, probably freaked out from all this confrontation. I used to be like that, but not anymore. After all—I'm wearing the huge ass diamond ring, not this woman.

"Why not?" she says. Well, no, she doesn't say it —she demands it.

I hold up my left hand. "Because Park doesn't have a girlfriend. He has a fiancé. And that's me."

Her nostrils flare. If it wasn't medically impossible, I'd be worried that fire might shoot out of her ears any second now.

"Wow," she says through clenched teeth. She blinks and stands a little taller, clearly trying hard to stay composed. "Congratulations on bribing the poor guy to marry you. It must be really scary to live each day knowing he's probably about you dumb you."

I laugh. "Oh sure, totally. I am positively terrified," I say with a big sarcastic smile. "You poor thing," I add, frowning. "You must be so tired making up so many lies to make yourself feel better. Anyhow, if you're not riding a dirt bike, you can leave now."

Then I give her my sweetest, most sugary smile. "Don't make me call the police to escort you out."

TWELVE
PARK

I'm so proud of my little eleven year old client, Jaxon. He's improved so much in the short while I've been giving him riding lessons. Many experts claim that older kids will never be able to turn into pro racers because they started learning how to ride too late in life. I think Jaxon has what it takes even though he's only been on a dirt bike for two years. Maybe he'll even be the first client I've trained that goes on to race professionally.

After his lesson is over, I check my phone and realize I have about an hour of unscheduled time before my next appointment. I'm going to go see if Becca wants to get lunch. I find her in the playroom with Jett. The two of them are laying in bean bags in front of the TV, watching a cartoon.

"Hey," I say, poking my head in the room.

Jett doesn't bother turning away from the TV.

Becca looks up. "Hey," she says, looking back at the TV. The colorful kid's cartoon doesn't seem that interesting, but she's watching it anyhow.

I sit on the floor next to her beanbag. "What's up?"

"Nothing," she says. "I'm tired but I'm too lazy to go home."

"Want to get some lunch with me?"

She shakes her head.

"You okay?" I ask.

"Yeah, just tired."

Something tells me she's feeling more than tired. It's probably wedding planning stress. Becca tries so hard not to let me know when things are bothering her, especially if those things are out of her control. I sit up on my knees then kiss the top of her head.

"You want me to drive you home?" I ask. "You could take a nap."

She shrugs. "Nah, I promised Bayleigh I'd hang out with Jett until she gets back from the store."

"I could take both of you back to our place?" I suggest. "Or back to their house?"

"No, I wanna stay here!" Jett says. He's still watching TV. Amazing how the kid pays attention to everything without looking like it.

"The kid has spoken," Becca says. She turns to me with a soft smile on her lips. I lean over and kiss her."

"Eww," Jett says.

"You're not even watching us!" I tease him.

"I can still hear you kissing!" he says back.

I laugh.

"You sure you're okay?" I ask Becca.

She nods. "Yep. Love you."

"I love you, too."

I still feel a little weird when I leave her with Jett, but Becca would tell me if something was really wrong. Maybe she is just tired. All I do know is that I'm still hungry. I walk over to the track and find Jace filling the tractor up with gas.

"Wanna get some lunch?"

Jace sets the five gallon gas jug on the ground and screws the cap back on the tractor. He's wearing swim shorts and a T-shirt with riding boots on his feet. It might look stupid to an outsider, but only people who work in the sun all day can truly understand how hot it gets in full riding gear. We wear the heavy duty riding boots to keep our legs safe from being burned from a dirt bike muffler, so it's worth it to look a little goofy every now and then.

"Is it lunch time already?" he says, checking his smart watch. "Damn, it's almost two? Where did the day go?"

I laugh. "Looks like you've been working hard for your paycheck."

"Tell me about it," he says. "I finally got that back tabletop jump the way I want it."

I peer out at the back corner of the track to the

jump he's talking about. Making a dirt bike track involves moving a lot of dirt and using a tractor to shape it into place. A tabletop jump is a long, flat stretch of dirt. The face of the jump is the most important; a steep face sends you straight up into the air, while a flatter face will send you soaring a long distance.

It looks good now. That jump had been a little too steep lately and now Jace has flattened it out. "So, lunch? I'm thinking tacos."

Jace's gaze looks behind me. His expression turns annoyed. "I hope that's for you and not me."

I turn around. A woman is walking up to us, trudging through the tall grass to where we are, which is a little annoying because we're off to the side of the track, in the outskirts where spectators don't go. She's wearing regular clothes so she's clearly not here to ride a dirt bike.

As she gets a little closer, I suddenly recognize her. She grins at me, and I struggle to remember her name.

"Angie?"

"Hi, Park," she says, taking a few steps to close the space between us.

"Phew," Jace says, indicating he's happy that she's here for me and not him. I want to punch him. Lucky bastard.

I haven't thought of this woman in years, but now that she's standing right here in front of me, I'm forced to remember how I know her. I think she's from Nebraska... or Tennessee. Her twin brother Andrew is a motocross racer who I grew up competing against on the regional level. He never made it past nationals, and once I turned pro, I ran into the two of them at quite a few races. Angie and I went on a date maybe once or twice. I can't really remember.

But I do remember I ended up blocking her number so she'd leave me alone. The girl is persistent.

"What are you doing here?" I ask.

Jace, my supposed best friend, suddenly finds himself busy with the tractor. Guess he's choosing to stay out of this conversation because he can spot trouble a mile away.

Angie flips her hair over her shoulder. "Oh, I'm just here with Andrew. He's trying out for the Houston race and thought he'd stop by and see your new track."

"Great," I say as I start to walk back toward the more populated area of the track. "Where's he parked? I'll go say hi."

"Don't worry about him," she says, reaching for my arm. I walk faster so she doesn't grab it. "I thought you'd be happier to see me."

I've been in this situation before. I know it sounds bad, and maybe it is bad. When you flirt with girls a lot, some of them get attached. I used to flirt all the time and it didn't mean anything to me. I just liked the attention.

Okay, yeah that is bad. I know. But I'm a changed man. I'm a one woman man. I have no desire to flirt with anyone who isn't my fiancé.

"How have you been?" I say. "You should meet my fiancé. She's great."

"I already did." Angie curls her lip. "Honey, you could do so much better than her."

"No, I can't, because she's perfect." I stop and face her, not breaking eye contact so she knows I'm serious. "There is no one better than my fiancé because she is absolutely perfect. And if you came here to start drama, you can just shut it down now. Because it's not happening."

She huffs a breath and opens her mouth but I turn away. I don't want to hear it.

"Excuse you!" she yells after me. "You and I had something special before you threw it away. I deserve another chance. Get back here and talk to me like a man!"

I stop. I don't think she deserves more of my time, but she's here on my home turf, and I feel the strong desire to put her in her place.

"We did not have anything special. You called and texted me so much I had to block your number. I'm sorry you're stuck on me when all we had was maybe one date, but it's done. It's over. You need to move on."

Angie folds her arms across her chest. "I can't believe she brainwashed you so much. If you were with me, you wouldn't have to quit motocross. I would just travel with you from city to city."

I laugh. "The best part of becoming an adult is realizing I don't have to listen to rude people. I don't have to give you my time or attention. Bye, Angie. Hope you find someone as manipulative as you are."

She spouts profanities back at me.

"Enjoy your stay in Texas!" I call back, giving a friendly wave behind me. Then I walk on toward the front of the track, fully content with my life and my choices.

THIRTEEN
BECCA

I tried really hard not to let that woman bother me, but my heart doesn't always listen to my mind. That's why I'm currently standing in the employee bathroom with an iPad, looking at the security cameras. With hair that bright, it's pretty easy to find her as I switch from one camera feed to the next, finally finding her walking toward the edge of the track. These cameras don't have sound, but I watch intently as she approaches Park and Jace. My heart pounds. I feel awful spying like this. But I also can't seem to look away.

I want to see how Park reacts to seeing her. Does he smile and hug her? Will he suddenly remember an old love and decide he wants her over me?

I can hear my heart racing in my ears and feel it thudding in my chest. She walks up. Park turns around.

He doesn't smile.

He definitely doesn't hug her.

Park looks annoyed.

My heart melts.

I was worried for nothing. I turn the camera app off and return to the playroom with Jett. My heart seriously needs to catch up with my brain. Because my brain knows that Park is no longer the player he was when I met him. My brain knows that Park is trustworthy and when he says I'm the only girl for him, he means it. It's my pesky heart that's always trying to protect me more than it should. It doesn't want me to believe the truth—it would rather keep me on guard.

I don't need to be on guard with Park. He's the man I'm going to marry. He's perfect.

I jump when my phone rings. I've been so heavily lost in thought that I kind of forgot I'm here in the playroom with Jett while he watches a movie. My mom is calling. I haven't talked to her much since I officially moved out a couple weeks ago. We send texts and stuff, but it's not like it used to be when I saw her almost every day.

"Hi, Mom," I say, answering the phone.

Jett rolls over on his side in the bean bag chair. I glance over at him. He's asleep, the little cutie pie. I get up and walk into the hallway so I won't wake him up. He played really hard this morning so he needs a good nap.

"Hey, kiddo. Are you at work?"

"Yeah, but I'm not really working so I can talk. What's up?"

"I was hoping you and Park could come over for Thanksgiving dinner this year."

"Oh, yeah of course."

I check the date on my phone. Thanksgiving is in a week. It's funny how I totally forgot about the holiday even though my house is fully decorated for it. I guess that's what happens when wedding planning takes over your life.

———

"HOW DO I LOOK?" Park asks. He slides his hands over the front of his dark green button up shirt. The color brings out the blue in his eyes and makes him look even more handsome. He's all fidgety as we walk up to my parent's front door.

"You look great," I say, reaching for his hand.

"I'm not too... casual?" He glances down. He's wearing a brand new pair of dark denim jeans, so it's not like they're his worn out holey ones with grease stains.

"It's dinner at my parents' house," I say, rolling my eyes. "This is not a fancy event. I'm sorry to break it to you, but the Queen will not be attending."

My parents aren't overly fancy or high maintenance. They'll just be happy to see us so it doesn't matter what we wear. Still, Park looks handsome as always. I'm wearing a maroon sweater dress I found at a thrift store for a total bargain. I love it, and it matches perfectly with my knee-high leather boots.

He smiles, but he still looks nervous. "I just want to impress them."

"They agreed to let you marry their daughter," I say with a snort. "Trust me, you've already impressed them."

I ring the doorbell. It feels like the right thing to do since I don't live here anymore... I shouldn't just walk right on in, right? Who knows. Becoming an adult is weird.

Mom opens the door and beams at us. She's wearing a denim dress with a brown belt around the waist and her hair is styled in a cute bun. She's bare-foot. I look over at Park, and hope he understands the look in my eyes. *See? There's nothing to worry about!*

"Happy Thanksgiving!" Mom says, squeezing us both in a hug. "Come in! I have appetizers out and the food will be ready in about thirty minutes."

My dad is on the couch watching football, but he stands to greet us. Then he and Park start talking about their favorite football teams and I leave them to talk while I hang out with Mom in the kitchen. Thanksgiving at our house has always been a nice, chill holiday. Sometimes my grandparents come over, but it's always a small gathering. Mom makes a roasted turkey, stuffing, mashed potatoes, her famous sweet rolls, and veggies covered in so much butter they're basically not a vegetable anymore.

Ever since I was old enough to help her in the kitchen, I've been here right beside her, helping make the meal. Now she's done it all without me. I feel a little bad.

"Mom, you should have called me sooner. I should have come over and helped cook."

"No," she says, waving my words away with the oven mitt on her hand. "I'm happy to make the meal. That's what grandparents do!"

I give her a side-eyed glance. "You're not a grandparent."

She pushes a tray of bacon-wrapped jalapeños toward me. "Not *yet*. But soon?"

The hopeful look in her eyes tells me she's more excited about becoming a grandmother than I ever knew. "Of course you'll be a grandparent someday," I say, reaching for a jalapeño. "But I need to get married first."

"I know, I know, but the wedding is less than two months away." She flashes me a grin as she drapes her apron over her neck and ties it in the back. "I'm just very excited for what's to come after!"

It's so sweet. I've never seen my mom like this. "What about Dad?" I ask. "Does he want to be a grandpa?"

"Oh honey, you have no idea." Mom laughs as she reaches into the fridge and takes out a bowl of green beans. "He's just as excited as I am. Raising kids is hard but being a grandparent will be the best! Bayleigh's mom can't brag enough about Jett. Soon I'll get to brag, too."

It's weird, this new existence. Not that long ago, I was a teenager. A kid. I lived here with my parents and they took care of me. Now I'm all grown up, and I'm about to be married. I'll have my own kids soon enough, and the cycle will continue. Sometimes the reality of life just hits me, like in moments like this.

I am all grown up. I have my own art business. I have an amazing fiancé. All that's missing is our future children.

And then life will be perfect.

I'm really starting to fit in with Becca's family. My own parents weren't always supportive, and I've never gotten along with them in the way that most people seem to get along with their parents. It's like I was one person and my parents were the complete opposite of me. I'm glad they're still in California.

Becca's dad is intimidating as hell but once he's out of the cop uniform, he's a pretty chill guy. He loves sports, so as long as I keep up with the football talk, he seems to like me. Becca's mom is really sweet. She's supportive and kind, and she's the kind of mom I wish I had. Having her as a mother-in-law will be the next best thing. I feel bad that Becca won't have a great mother-in-law, but it's in everyone's best interest that we stay away from my parents. Becca has only met them once at Christmas, and it was a total disaster.

I shrug away the thoughts and look over at my beautiful bride to be. After having Thanksgiving lunch with the Sosa Family, we came back home to relax.

"This is our last Thanksgiving as boyfriend and girlfriend," I say, stretching my arm around her shoulders while we sit on the couch.

"Technically, that was last year," she says. "This year is our last Thanksgiving as fiancés."

I make a *tisk* sound. "You are as clever as you are beautiful."

She rolls her eyes and snuggles up closer to me. I've learned when to anticipate those eye rolls of hers. She does it every time I compliment her. Both of our phones buzz at the same time from the coffee table.

I have a text from Jace. It simply says: FRIENDSGIVING.

"What the heck is Friendsgiving?" Becca says, looking at her phone. She turns the screen to face me. Bayleigh has texted her the exact same thing.

I call Jace on speakerphone.

"Dude. We just watched some boring ass girl movie—"

He's interrupted by Bayleigh in the background —"It was a romantic comedy!"

"—yeah, yeah, same difference," Jace continues. "They had a Friendsgiving. It's like Thanksgiving but with friends only so no family drama. Y'all need to come over now. Friendsgiving is about to begin."

"But don't you have to cook food for something like that?" Becca asks.

"We're getting takeout," Bayleigh says. "Come over!"

"Nowwwww," Jace crones into the phone. Then the call ends.

"They're not even drinking," I say with a laugh.

Becca stands up and stretches her arms over her head. "Guess we're eating two big meals today."

I pat my stomach. "No complaints here."

I wear the same clothes I've been wearing all day because I'm already dressed nice. Becca changes her leather boots for a pair of sandals. It's cool outside and it's already starting to get dark even though it's just before seven o'clock, so I drive us to their house instead of walking.

"Welcome!" Jace says, meeting us at the door. "To the first annual Friendsgiving."

"Next year we'll plan it better," Bayleigh says. She's also wearing a dress that looks like it's made out of one big sweater, but it's blue. She and Becca immediately gush over how they're "twins". I don't know why, but I'm suddenly remembering this one girl I dated for a summer back when I was around sixteen. Jace's girlfriend at the time hated my girl-friend. We could never do anything fun together because the girls didn't get along. This is just another reason I know Becca is the perfect girl. She's best friends with my best friend's wife.

The Adams' living room is a mess of Jett's toys, but Bayleigh has decorated the dining room for a party. There are wine glasses, boxed wine, and a ridiculous amount of takeout food. I spot Chinese food, pizza, tacos, and mini cupcakes from that place in town that the girls love.

"You guys went all out," I say, taking a slice of pizza.

"We were both exhausted with family stuff, and we thought it would be fun to celebrate with our friends," Bayleigh says.

Jett comes running into the room making *"vroom vroom"* sounds while he holds a toy dirt bike in the air. That kid only has one speed—running. His eyes widen at the food all spread out on the table. "Can I have pizza?"

"Of course you can," Jace says. He scoops up his toddler and hands him a slice of pizza. With Jett on his hip, Jace looks at me. "You need to come see my vision."

"Huh?"

Bayleigh leans over his shoulder and explains, "He has a vision for how he wants the back yard to look."

"You mean you don't like having a dirt bike track back there?" I snort.

"I mean the *immediate* back yard," he says. Jett

holds his pizza slice close to Jace's mouth and he takes a bite. For whatever reason, Jett thinks this is hilarious. Kids are cute. And weird.

We follow them out the back door. There's a small deck back here, and then it's just grass with Jett's swing set to the left. Beyond that is the tiny bicycle track that Jett pretends is a real dirt bike track.

"Picture this," Jace says. He sets Jett on the ground and then holds out his hands. "One big ass pool."

Jett's eyes widen and he pops his hand over his mouth. "Daddy said a bad word!" he whispers, but he's a kid so his form of a whisper is basically a normal voice.

"Yes, he did," Bayleigh says in her mommy voice. She turns her gaze to her husband. "Daddy's in trouble now."

"Oops," Jace says. "Let me try that again... picture this... one big-butted pool."

I laugh so hard I almost choke on my pizza.

"A pool would be awesome," Becca says.

"Right?" Jace walks out into the yard. He describes his vision to us—a large deck with one of those built in outdoor kitchens. Then decorative stonework that leads to a huge saltwater pool. "We could get one of those waterfall things too. And a hot tub."

"I am all about the hot tub," Bayleigh says, gazing

off to the grassy spot Jace designated as the future pool.

"So when is this backyard paradise happening?" I ask.

"I have some people coming out next week to give me estimates. Hopefully by next summer it'll be done."

"Sweet." I haven't been swimming in a long time, but now the idea of a pool to jump into after a long day of working in the hot sun sounds like heaven. If he didn't live right next to me, maybe I'd have to get a pool too. As it is, I can just mooch off of Jace.

Back inside, I eat entirely too much food. I'll have to work out twice a day for a week to burn it all off. But the wine is good and the company is even better. Jett ends up falling asleep in my lap on the floor where we had been playing with his toy dirt bikes. I don't dare get up because I don't want to wake him.

But I don't mind at all. This kid is my godson, and he's one of my favorite people on earth. I can't wait to see who he'll grow up to be.

FIFTEEN
BECCA

On Sunday, I spend the day packing my latest orders so I can take them to the post office tomorrow morning. My little art shop called Becca's Inspirations is doing well. I started out selling on Etsy, but now I have my own website and I get more business from that, which makes me feel like an official business owner. Selling on Etsy always felt more like a hobby. When I start feeling like an official business owner, I start realizing I know absolutely nothing about business.

And then I always come back to the idea of college. There was a time when I wanted to be a pharmacy technician. Then I wanted to get the basic classes out of the way so I could study art. I hated all of it. Now I can't stop thinking that if I'm ever going to succeed with my own business, or with working at The Track, I'll need to go back to college.

So once again I open my laptop and research colleges near me. There are small colleges and big colleges and online colleges all offering business degrees. Some of them are quite expensive. Would having a college degree make me a better business-woman? A better person? A better wife?

I've already failed at graduating before. I didn't fail my classes... I just gave up. I don't want to start college again only to give up yet again. That's worse than never going.

I sit in my studio a long time researching colleges. I pull my transcripts and compare how many credits I have to how many I'd need for a bachelor's degree. It's a lot. Seeing how much work it would take to graduate makes my stomach hurt and my shoulders fall. I feel defeated before I've even started.

There's a slight knock on the studio door.

"Babe?" Park says. "You fall asleep in there?"

"I'm awake," I call out.

He walks in looking all cute in his black pajama pants and white undershirt. I glance at the time on my laptop. It's just after midnight.

"I didn't realize it was so late," I say, standing up and closing my laptop. "Sorry."

"No worries." Park gazes at the packages on the floor. "Wow, that's a lot of orders."

"Selling prints of my original artwork was a

really good idea. I made six hundred dollars this week."

"Nice," he says. "What are you gonna buy me with all that cash?"

I smack his butt as I walk past him to the stairs. "You wish."

He follows me down to our bedroom, which looks so much better now that I live here. Instead of an old plain comforter and ugly sheets, we have all nice new bedding and matching bedroom furniture. I hung up framed photos of us and set out vanilla scented candles on the nightstand. My favorite artwork, however, is the canvas Park painted, asking me to marry him. I have it on the wall next to my dresser. My new room is vastly different than my childhood bedroom. It's mature and simple and clean.

And I get to share it with Park.

I crawl into our huge bed and then slide over until I'm in the middle of the mattress. Park turns on his side, facing me with his head propped up on his hand. "I get to marry you in a month."

I smile. "Yes you do."

His hand slides gently down my face then settles on my hip. "You'll be Mrs. Becca Park."

Sometimes I forget his real name is Nolan Park and everyone calls him his last name. I love both of his names and I'm thrilled to be changing my last name to his.

I snuggle closer to him under the blankets. His hand slides down and grabs my butt. Sometimes I wake up in the middle of the night and he's holding me just like this.

"One more month..." I say softly as my head rests against his chest. I lean up and kiss his collarbone. His hand tightens on my butt. I have to concentrate to speak. "Pretty much all of the wedding plans are done." I kiss him again and he lets out a soft little sigh.

"Now we just have one last thing to do before the wedding." His voice is deep and sultry and it awakens a heat in my belly.

"What's that?" I say, lifting my head up a bit to look at him in the glow of the lamplight.

He wiggles his eyebrows suggestively. "The bachelor and bachelorette parties."

I smile. "Is it weird that I'm not really that excited for it because I'll miss you while I'm out with my friends?"

"Nope, I feel the same way." He kisses me, letting his tongue slide across my bottom lip. He knows that's exactly what it takes to turn me on. "But I have to go or Jace will be so upset."

I chuckle between kissing him and letting our tongues explore each other. Our bodies are pressed tightly together, and I can feel every single inch of him pressed up against me. "We'll make the most of the parties and then come back home to each other."

His teeth gently bite my neck just before he kisses me. My breathing gets harder as my whole body lights up under his delicate touch.

"I know something we can make the most of," he breathes. With one strong movement, he rolls me on top of him then settles his hands back over my butt.

"What's that?" I say with a giggle.

Just before his lips close over mine, he whispers, "Tonight."

SIXTEEN
PARK

We're two hours into the drive to Lake Conroe when Dustin pops his head up into the front seat. "Yo, why are bachelor parties supposed to celebrate your last night of freedom when it's really not the last night because the wedding is still in two weeks?"

Dustin is one of my oldest friends from Texas. He's also the most inquisitive.

"I have no idea," I say, glancing at Jace who is in the driver's seat. The three of us make up probably the smallest bachelor party ever, but I only wanted my best friends with me for the weekend.

"I used to think bachelor parties happened the day before the wedding," Jace says. "At least that's what it seems like on TV, but that's a bad idea because you can't be all hungover the morning of your wedding."

"It's a symbolic party of the end of your bachelor days," I say.

Dustin nods and leans back into the large backseat, stretching out his arms across the back of the seat. "Makes sense."

Sometimes Becca asks me what us guys talk about when we're hanging out at the track. I think she thinks all we do is talk about hot girls or sex, but she'd be wrong. Sometimes we talk about stupid shit like this.

It's the weekend before Christmas. Since next weekend is Christmas and a few days after that is our wedding, this is the best time to have the bachelor party. Jace, Dustin, and I are heading to Lake Conroe for some outdoor fun on the lake. It's winter here so we got a great price on a luxury resort suite. It's some place called Camp Canyon and it's advertised as a luxury hotel for the outdoorsman. Whatever that means, since true outdoorsmen usually don't care about luxury.

"How much longer do we have?" I ask. Absentmindedly, I reach for my pocket, and then sigh. "That's right... someone stole my phone."

"Just for the weekend," Jace says. "You know the rules. No calling your fiancé until the party is over."

It's a stupid rule, but Becca and I agreed to it. Not being able to talk to each other for a whole weekend is supposed to be some cutesy way to miss each other before the wedding. It's not like I can't spend time with my friends without her – but I'd much prefer being able to talk to her when I need to. What if something happens and she needs me?

It's a shame that Jace and Bayleigh had a dual party when they got married. I wish I could have tortured him the way he's torturing me.

Dustin pulls up the resort on his phone. "We're twelve miles away."

"Sweet."

I spend the rest of the drive feeling angsty about not having my phone. I try to forget about it, but it's weird not having that lifeline to Becca whenever I need her. At least I can take some comfort in knowing that if I get injured on a jet ski, Jace will be here to call her for me.

Lake Conroe has beautiful deep blue water and some great views. Half the lake is taken up by private properties that are million dollar mansions over-looking the water. The other half is open to the public. Camp Canyon is on the north side of the lake, sprawling over dozens of acres of greenery that overlooks the lake. The resort has horseback riding, fishing, boat and jet ski rentals, and a large pool with a swim up bar. There are also random outdoor games around the grounds like cornhole, a bean bag tossing game, and golf, volleyball, and a basketball court.

The woman at the front desk tells us about all of these amenities when we check in. She gives me a brochure that I flip through on the elevator ride up to the top floor where our fancy suite awaits.

"I already know I want to bring Becca here one day," I say, as I look over the list of all the things there is to do here. You can have a complete vacation without ever leaving the property. "They even have a spa with couples massages. Becca would love it here."

"No talking about Becca," Dustin says. "That's the rules."

"I'll get a couples massage with you," Jace says with a sarcastic snort.

The elevator dings and the doors open. Our suite is one of only four rooms on this floor—that's how big it is.

There are two bedrooms in this suite, as well as a living room and full kitchen. The patio stretches the length of the hotel room, giving an amazing view of the lake. Everything is decorated in this masculine lodge type style. There's leather furniture and fur rugs and a big huge fireplace made of stones. I expect to turn the corner and see some wealthy oil tycoon signing contracts and smoking a cigar.

Jace and I decide to share the largest room and we give the smaller room to Dustin. Jace says he's fine crashing on the massive leather couch, but knowing him, he'll probably end up passing out fully clothed on the bed next to me. We're not into anything wild and crazy, so there won't be strippers or other debauchery at this party.

Except for the booze.

"Gentleman," Dustin says, opening the stainless steel refrigerator. "Looks like my custom order has been filled."

The whole fridge is full of liquor, at least ten bottles which is more than enough for the three of us.

"Nice," Jace says, fist-bumping him. "But first thing's first—" He points a finger at me. "Jet skis?"

"Jet skis," I say.

"In December?" Dustin squeaks. "It's cold out there, bro!"

I shrug. "You brought your wetsuit, right?"

Dustin snorts. "I'm a BMXer, dude. I don't do wetsuits."

Jace tosses the hotel key card to him. "You can be the photographer. Take lots of photos for the Gram."

HOURS LATER, Jace and I are frozen to the bone, but it's worth it. We love renting jet skis. One of these days we'll buy our own and go to the lake all the time. Sadly, there's only so much time for recreational activities when you're the boss of your own company.

After we're dressed and back in the hotel, Dustin shows off the photos he took. We also played some pool in the fancy game room downstairs before coming up here and ordering dinner. Tomorrow we'll try all the other outdoor events they have. Maybe even some horseback riding. It's my bachelor party, after all—might as well go all out and enjoy every second of it.

Dustin gets to work mixing drinks at our hotel bar. Jace and I open the sliding glass doors that go out onto the balcony and turn on the outdoor heaters. It's not too cold out tonight, but it's cold enough to need the sweatpants I packed, and maybe some socks too.

We play some music and hang out, play cards, and slowly get drunk. It's fun, don't get me wrong.

I just really miss my girl.

"Stop thinking of the wifey!" Jace says, throwing a card at me. He picks up his glass and downs the rest of his whiskey. "This is a guys' only night."

"You've talked to Bayleigh twice," I say. "You should at least let me call Becca just once."

He shakes his head. "No can do."

"Rules are rules," Dustin says. He leans over and refills Jace's glass from the whiskey jar that sits in the middle of the table.

I deal another round of cards for a game of poker. I miss her so bad, but I'm trying not to act like it. No need to give my friends more fuel to make fun of me.

Jace beats us in three rounds of poker. I don't know how the guy always has such good luck, but at least we're not betting any actual money on these games.

"I gotta piss," I say, standing up. The blood rushes to my head and I realize I'm a little drunker than I thought I was. Maybe I should eat some more pizza. I stumble my way into the bedroom, then turn to the bathroom to pee. Jace's phone sits on the counter.

I pick it up, seizing my opportunity, and call Becca.

"Hey, is everything okay?" she answers.

"It's me," I say.

"Hi, babe. Why are you on Jace's phone?"

"He took my phone away from me," I say, lowering my voice to a whisper so Jace doesn't hear me. I need to make this quick because he might remember his phone is in here. "I'm not supposed to talk to my beautiful bride at my bachelor party."

She laughs. "Bayleigh just told me to stay off my phone but she didn't take it away."

"I miss you." I whisper.

"I miss you," she says back all sweetly. I can picture how damn beautiful she looks right now. She always looks beautiful.

"I'm a little drunk," I mumble into the phone.

"I can tell that," she says in the cutest, lightest little voice. God, I love her so much.

"I love you," I say.

"I love you."

"I can't wait to marry you."

She giggles. "Since when do you get all sappy when you've been drinking?"

"I just really, really miss you."

"Well, I have some really good news for you."

I turn on the sink so it sounds like I'm washing my hands. Then I realize I should probably actually wash my hands. "What's that?"

"You get to spend the rest of your life with me."

I grin. "Lucky me."

SEVENTEEN

BECCA

Planning a bachelorette party during December isn't exactly a *bad* idea... but it's not a good idea to have it at a beach. Maybe some kind of ski lodge in the snowy mountains would be more ideal, but we live in Texas, and here in Texas we go to the beach. I love the beach. I know it's not the most beautiful here because our sand is this dingy brown color and the water is an even worse brown. Nasty old seaweed washes up on the shore. When you picture a beach, you think of white sand and blue water that's so clear you can see your feet as you wade into it. Maybe one day Park and I will go to Hawaii and experience all those picturesque views.

For now, I'm hanging out with my best friend in a huge beach house we got for a great price. During the summer, these things rent fast and for as high as seven hundred dollars a night. But now, a week before Christmas, we got our four bedroom two story gorgeously renovated beach house for just three hundred dollars for the whole weekend.

Bayleigh wanted to have a party where we invite every girlfriend we have, but I decided I'd rather just hang out with her. The wedding is almost here. I've been working nonstop on Becca's Inspirations trying to grow my business online. I've also been researching colleges and looking into business degrees. I've been so busy lately that all I want to do is chill out.

Bayleigh is the best. It takes about an hour to get to this part of the Texas coast and we drove together. But when we walked into the beach house I was shocked to find it already decorated. There were blue and silver streamers, confetti, and balloons making the gorgeous beach house look even better. She said she'd called the owner and offered to pay a bit more if they'd set up the decorations before we arrived.

The house is right on the beach. You park on the concrete slab underneath the house and then walk up a flight of stairs outside to get to the front door. All the homes on this part of the beach are built up high on beams to prevent flooding during hurricanes. Once you're inside, you're greeted with beautiful beach-themed décor. Not tacky stuff like taxidermy fish hanging on the wall, but serene wooden mermaids, seashells, and blue-green sea glass artwork. The entire back wall of the house—the wall that faces the beach—is made of floor to ceiling windows, giving you an amazing view of the ocean. The houses are spaced far apart so you don't feel like any of the neighbors can see you when you walk out to the beach. It's amazing. I want us to all come back here as couples in the summertime.

"Dinner is served, my lady," Bayleigh says in this exaggerated British accent.

"Who are you trying to be?" I ask as I stand up from the couch. "Harry Potter?" She had insisted on cooking all the meals yesterday, and today I helped her with breakfast and lunch but she wanted to make dinner. Something about treating me like royalty since it's my bachelorette party.

"I am your humble house servant," she says, waving a spatula at me. "Like on Downton Abbey."

"Ahh," I say, making may way over to the kitchen table. It's a long marble table that seats twelve people and faces the windows. "Well in that case, you're doing a terrible job. Servants should be seen, not heard."

"Yes, yes, of course, my lady," she says.

We burst out laughing.

Bayleigh brings both our plates of food over to the table. We sit on the same side so we can look out at the beach. The weather is calm today, so only gentle waves crest on shore. The sun is slowly starting to set behind us, casting beautiful orange rays onto the water.

She's made chicken stir fry with veggies and it smells amazing. I take one bite, and it *is* amazing.

"Um, hello? When did you learn to cook so well?" I say, shoving another bite of food in my mouth. Yesterday she'd made us French toast for breakfast, cheeseburgers for lunch, and a Mexican casserole for dinner. They were all delicious.

"YouTube and lots of trial and error," she says with a laugh. "I realized I'm sick of being bad a cooking so I've been practicing lately. To be fair though, these meals I've made for you are basically all I know how to make."

"I could live off this stir fry for the rest of my life," I say, stabbing my fork into a piece of chicken. "You have to teach me. I need to be a good wife who knows how to cook."

"Yeah, right," Bayleigh says. "Park isn't some macho asshole who wants a woman in the kitchen. He'll be right next to you helping you cook."

I smile, because she's right. Park has told me numerous times that I don't have to work if I don't want to. He's also told me that we're partners and he doesn't want a wife to just wait on him hand and foot.

"I still need to learn how to cook," I say. "It's all part of being an adult, I suppose."

She nods. "There's still like five million things I

need to learn about being an adult. Did you know you have to call around and price check your car insurance, house insurance, and electricity bill every freaking year so you don't get ripped off?

I lift an eyebrow. "I barely know how to sign up for those services."

She laughs. "Exactly. I've been listening to podcasts about finances and stuff. I guess I feel like some utter failure for being a teen mom with no college education. I don't want to be dumb. I want to be an adult who has their life together, ya know?"

"You are an adult," I say, smiling at her. "And you and Jace have built an amazing life."

"Oh, crap!" She stands up. "I almost forgot the wine!" she says in her British accent. She scurries over to the kitchen in her socked feet and then returns with a new bottle of Rosé and two wine glasses. This house came equipped with dishes and cooking stuff but no food. We brought all of that ourselves.

I decide to put on a haughty accent as well. I peer down my nose at her. "How dare you forget my wine, Miss Pennyfeather. I shall dock your pay this week as punishment."

"Pennyfeather?" Bay says, laughing. "What kind of name is that?"

"I dunno," I say, laughing as she pours my glass my of wine. "It sounded fancy."

After we eat, we put on our matching bridal

hoodies and head out onto the balcony. The hoodies are blue with silver writing on the front. Bay had them made just for us. Mine says Bride and hers says Maid of Honor. Underneath that is my wedding date.

We sit on the balcony watching the sun set and the waves crash on shore. Bay makes sure our wine glasses are never empty. I love the sound of the beach. The water, the seagulls, the soft sound of the nature all around us. There's not another person in sight, and I love it. Usually the beaches are packed with people, but that's in the summer. Coming here during the winter is something special. It's like this part of the world only belongs to us.

"Bay?" I say, looking over at her after a few moments of silence.

"Yes, my lady," she says, grinning at me.

"How does married life change you?"

She tilts her head. "You having second thoughts?"

"No, not at all." I think of Park and smile. "It's just... weird... and it's so much all at once. I used to be a girlfriend and I'm about to be a wife. I'm worried things won't be as romantic and fun if we become a boring old married couple."

Bay opens her mouth like she's about to say something, then she stops. She thinks for a moment. "Well.... Yeah, it does get boring sometimes. Like, you get married and it's exciting and then you just slip into normal life. But that's not a bad thing. There's something really comforting about having Jace. I just..." She takes a deep breath and looks out at the beach, then turns back to me. "It's like... he's my soul mate. My other half. I never have to worry. I don't care about all the women who obsess over him online. I don't care about his exes. I know it's just me and Jace, forever and ever. And I can't describe how great that is. I know that if I have trouble with Jett, he's right there. If my car gets a flat tire, I can call him. I never have to *worry*."

I nod, watching her talk. The look on her face almost says more than her words do. She's happy. She's content. She's not the least bit worried about her life.

She refills her glass of wine. "So much of life is out of your control, but when you're married to your soul mate, you have someone with you. Even on the boring normal days where nothing happens, something is still happening—you're living your life with your husband. It's totally worth it, I promise."

I feel a warmth deep in my chest. If there was ever a perfect relationship in this world, it's Jace and Bayleigh's. "I hope Park and I will be as happy as you guys are."

"Pshh," she says. "You will. Park is crazy in love with you and he's a really good guy." She holds up her glass toward me. "We're going to be the coolest, happiest, married best friends ever."

"I'll toast to that," I say, tapping my glass to hers.

A cold breeze picks up, blasting us with a chill. Bayleigh reaches over her shoulder and flips the switch that turns on the outdoor heater. "I wonder what the boys are up to."

"Probably freezing their ass off on jet skis."

She nods. "And acting like they're too macho to come inside to warm up."

I lean back in my patio chair, kicking my feet up on the whicker ottoman in front of me. "They're not smart like we are. We have warm hoodies and wine."

"They have junk food and jet skis. We are clearly more sophisticated."

We grin and we click our glasses together again.

I think of Park and how sweet it was when he called me last night after sneaking Jace's phone. He sounded all sad and lonely and I could tell he really missed me. I miss him too, of course, but I also enjoy this relaxing time with my best friend.

"Those boys are lucky to have us," Bayleigh says.

"Yep. Good thing they know it."

EIGHTEEN
PARK

Christmas went by in a blur. Becca and I decorated our very first tree together. The smell of fresh pine filled up the house with Christmas spirit. We exchanged gifts and had a great time at her parent's house for a Christmas Eve dinner. On Christmas morning, we went to Jace and Bayleigh's and watched Jett open all his presents from Santa. Christmas is so much more fun when there's a kid around. Christmas is magical to kids. It made me realize how badly I want to have my own kids to share this holiday with.

But now the holiday is over and the countdown to my wedding is on. Only five more days until Becca and I exchange our vows, and I couldn't be more excited. Technically, the business is closed all week, opening again on January 3rd, but I'm here in my office catching up on paperwork. If only running a motocross track meant riding dirt bikes all day.

Instead, it's more like riding dirt bikes in the tiny bits of free time you find between training clients, working on the dirt with the tractor, calling vendors and suppliers, scheduling clients, talking to parents, and figuring out taxes and payroll. I finally solved the payroll problem by finding JR Bookkeeping to help me with paychecks. He has a great website where I enter in the employee's work hours and info, and he calculates all the taxes for me and handles printing the paychecks. One of these days we'll get all fancy with it and do direct deposit.

I turn in my office chair to the coffee maker in the corner of my office, refilling my mug. I have two more hours to work before I head into town for my final tuxedo fitting for the wedding. They had warned me not to gain or lose any weight to make sure it fits me well on my wedding day. Hopefully all that junk food and beer we had at the bachelor party didn't make me fat.

Just before I'm about to pack up and head to the tuxedo shop, I get a call on my cell phone.

"Hello, Mr. Park. I'm afraid we have a problem with your tuxedo rental."

"What's going on?" I ask, standing up and grabbing my truck keys.

"We can't find it."

"What?"

"I'm so sorry, sir. I had it two days ago and now it's gone. I've been calling every employee trying to find out where it went." The woman on the other end of the line sounds absolutely horrified to be talking to me with this bad news, so I hold back and don't say anything rude. But I'm getting a bit horrified myself.

"What are the odds that you'll find it?"

"I don't know. But your fitting is today so we can try on other tuxedos as well."

I thank her for her help in solving this problem. But inside, I'm a wreck as I drive over there. Jace and I spent three hours trying on tuxedos to find a good one. I never expected to care about something like this, but I realized our wedding photos will be memorized forever and I don't want to look back and see myself wearing an ugly or ill-fitted tux.

At the store, the woman who greets me is the same one who helped me pick out the tux two months ago. She looks like she's about to cry at any second.

"I'm so, so, sorry, Mr. Park." There's a fine crease between her eyes as she pleads with me. "I just tracked it down. A new salesman gave the suit to someone else for the week and we won't get it back in time."

"It's okay," I say soothingly, hoping she doesn't cry. "These things happen."

Her expression goes from terrified to relieved in

an instant. I am actually freaking out myself, but I don't want her to know that. Plus, the more worried I get, the worse everything will be. I take a deep breath. "What other suits do you have?"

She leads me to the row of tuxedos and my heart drops. I have flashbacks of the day I spent here trying on every damn thing they had, only to finally find the tux I liked. I already know there's nothing here that I want. I think I tried them all on last time.

I walk down the row of tuxedos to the rack that's in my size. There's no time for alterations now, she tells me. We'll have to find something off the rack that works. But I already know none of them work. I want to look like a male model, not like some random dude in a tux.

"I'm so sorry," she says again. "I told my manager. I hope he fires that idiot who rented your tux. I had the order slip and everything on it and he just took it off and gave it to someone else!"

"It's okay," I say. "My wedding will still be perfect even if I look bad."

She smiles. "Aww. That's so sweet."

I rub my hand over my face. "Okay, let's get started trying these things on."

Another woman rushes up to us holding a black garment bag draped over her arm. "Melissa!" she says to the woman helping me. Then she whispers something to her.

Melissa's eyes light up. She looks from the garment bag to me.

"It's his size," the other woman says.

Melissa grins. She takes the garment and carries it over to the fitting room. "Follow me," she tells me. "I think I have the perfect tux."

She talks to me through the fitting room curtain while I strip down to my boxers and pull on the pants and then the black button up shirt. I know from experience that she'll help me put on the rest of the suit, and make sure my tie looks good. Melissa tells me this is a one of a kind designer suit that just came in. It's never been worn and the rental price is four times what I paid for mine, but she will rent it to me for the same price as my old one, plus a discount for the inconvenience.

"I think it'll look great on you," she says. "It's very contemporary."

I'm already liking what I see as I slip into the tux. I open the curtain and Melissa helps me finish out the suit with the vest thing and the jacket. She grins widely and steps back to admire me. "Look in the mirror," she says.

I turn around. The suit is jet black. Every single part of it. It has a narrow collar and tie. Melissa takes a midnight blue silk tie and holds it up to my neck. "You could even wear this one to match your wedding colors. What do you think?"

I barely recognize the man in the mirror. I'm not

exactly vain or into fashion, but even I can admit that I look amazing. I look sexy as hell.

I watch my face in the mirror as a grin slides on my lips. Behind me, Melissa presses her hands together in front of her chest. "It's perfect, right?"

"Yes," I say, turning to her. "I finally look worthy enough to stand next to my bride."

I TAKE the new tux home with me since the wedding is so close and we don't want to risk losing it again before the wedding. Most rentals are only for two days, but Melissa made an exception and gave me this one for a week. There's a part of me that wants to walk around wearing this damn thing all day, every day, until I have to return it. That's how good I look in it.

I don't recognize the blue Mazda car in my driveway when I get home, but Becca's car is here too so I'm guessing it's someone wedding related. Over the past few weeks we've had our photographer, the caterer, and the custom wedding invitation person over at our house, so it's all par for the course to find strange cars here.

When I walk in, I hear Bayleigh and another woman's voice. They're set up in the kitchen. There are makeup boxes and hair spray and curling irons and stuff all over the granite countertop. I realize the tall woman with blonde hair must be Bayleigh's Aunt Truly who is doing Becca's hair and makeup for the wedding. Bayleigh and the woman styling Becca's hair are currently blocking her from my view. She's sitting in director style chair, and all I can see is her leggings and flip flops.

"Hi, ladies," I say to let them know I'm here.

Bayleigh waves. "Do you want to see look number one?"

"Yes, even though I have no idea what that means."

Both women step out of the way. Bayleigh says something about how they tried three different hair and makeup styles today but are pretty sure they want to go with the first option, which Becca is wearing now. I barely hear a word she says.

Because my future wife is stunning.

"Oh my God," I breathe. My whole body seems to go numb as I stand here, mouth agape and heart pounding, watching her. She gives me a sheepish grin. Her hair is all done up in some fancy way with sparkly bobby pins or whatever in it. Her makeup is done in such a way to make her look like a real live angel. Like she came straight from Heaven.

"You are so beautiful," I say. I don't even think I blink. I can't take my eyes off her.

I walk up and reach for her hand. She smiles up at me. "You sure? Is this how I should look on our wedding day?"

I nod. "I didn't think it was possible for you to be any more beautiful."

Becca's cheeks flush. She turns to the makeup lady. "Thank you, Aunt Truly. Getting that reaction from him tells me you're the greatest makeup artist in the world."

She chuckles. "I aim to please."

"So is that your tux?" Becca asks, nodding to the black garment bag that's still in my hand. I nod. "There was a slight problem at the store, but it worked out for the best."

"I wish I could see it," she says.

"Not until the wedding day," Bayleigh chirps. She turns to me. "But that doesn't mean I can't see it. You have photos, right?"

"Yep." I'd taken maybe a little too many selfies while wearing the tux today. I take out my phone and we turn away from Becca, who playfully groans about being left out. I show the photos to Bayleigh.

Her jaw drops. "Damn, son!"

She turns around and winks at Bayleigh. "Your future husband is a hottie."

NINETEEN

BECCA

The air smells like cinnamon from the candles on the table and pine from the wood panels on the walls. It's a crisp, beautiful day, and it's the last day of the year. In just a few short hours, I will be getting married.

I'll be Mrs. Nolan Park.

A giddy excitement flows through me. I think it's been flowing through me all week. It's like my blood has been replaced with happiness. I'm in one of the tree houses with my mom, grandma, Bayleigh, and Aunt Truly. Park and the guys are in another treehouse. Our photographer Clara snaps photos every few minutes, capturing memories of the bridal party while we get dressed and ready. Every now and then she walks over to the other treehouse to get pictures of the guys.

We're watching sappy romantic Christmas movies on the large television in the living room and drinking hot apple cider. Last night we met with the pastor who is marrying us and we timed out our rehearsal, so now we know it takes exactly six minutes for me to walk down the aisle and exchange vows with Park. Because of this, our wedding will start at six minutes before midnight.

Our guest list is under twenty people, but they are the people who mean the most to us, so this is a special, perfect night. Just like the bachelorette beach house rental, this treehouse has a balcony, but it's much smaller. When I step out onto the balcony, I'm greeted by a large tree branch. The porch was built around it, leaving the existing tree intact. I place my hand on the bark and stare out at the river below. Park's tree house is just across the way, and between the houses are the chairs and aisle below. The aisle is just the grass on the ground, but they've decorated each side with a line of white rose petals. There's also a white archway that's carved out of wood at the end of the aisle. When Park and I say our vows, we'll be standing in front of the gorgeous river. With all this nature around me, I almost feel like a fairy. All I need is wings.

We lucked out with the weather today. It's cool, but not cold, and no humidity in sight. All you need is a sweater or shawl and you'll be fine outside. Plus the grounds have outdoor heaters as well. The whole thing is cozy and beautiful after the sun sets. Clear lights are strung up all between the treehouses. It's like a magic fairy tale down below.

"I think it's time for the dress," Mom says, checking her watch. She's wearing a dark blue satin gown with a silver shawl. Aunt Truly did her hair as well, so it's pulled up in a soft updo with little fringes of hair framing her face.

"Really?" I say, walking back inside. I check my reflection in the big mirror on the kitchen counter. Aunt Truly brought her own mirrors since the treehouses don't have professional makeup booths in them.

"It's twenty five minutes till you go out there," Mom says. When we timed getting my dress on last night, it took about ten minutes. Lacing up the bodice on my gown is a big affair that takes at least two people. We budgeted extra time today in case anything goes wrong.

I exhale, feeling my heart speed up. It's almost time. In the mirror, I see someone youthful and elegant staring back at me. I love my hair. It's been curled in big waves, and the top half is pulled back and held in place with a rhinestone tiara. My makeup looks absolutely perfect because Aunt Truly is a genus.

I turn to my family. "Let's do this."

We get my gown on and I wear my flip flops for the journey down the rope bridge and spiraling staircases to the ground while Bayleigh holds my heels.

She's wearing her Maid of Honor dress, which I let her pick out so she'd be happy with it. It's the same shade of midnight blue as Mom's dress, but it's much sexier. It's long and slinky and fits her body like a glove. I can't wait to see all the pictures Clara takes tonight because this might be the best we've ever looked.

The treehouses have planned ahead for weddings where the bride and the groom can't see each other beforehand. One of the employees checks with us to make sure we're ready and then he goes over to Park's treehouse and makes sure he doesn't leave so he won't see me.

Then we make our way down to the ground. It takes a long time making sure my gorgeous dress doesn't get snagged on any of the greenery or wooden stairs. At the bottom, there's a cute little mini log cabin set up as a waiting room. Since it's dark outside, we sneak across the grass, behind all the wedding guests who are facing the river, oblivious to our presence.

Once inside the log cabin, I find myself out of breath. I don't know why—nerves, I guess. I sit on the big chaise lounge in here while Bayleigh peeks out the small window.

"The boys are getting in position!" She puts a hand to her chest. "Jett is the cutest ring bearer!"

"Let me see!" I peek out the window and watch our little Jett walk down the aisle in his adorable tuxedo. We didn't know a little girl so we just decided not to have a flower girl. But that's okay because Jett totally steals the show.

My nerves ramp up. Mom squeezes my hand. "You look so beautiful, honey. I'm so happy for you."

"Thanks, Mom." I give her a tight hug.

And then there's a knock on the door. They're ready for us.

Mom checks her watch. "Right on time!" She gives me a soft kiss on the cheek so as to not mess up my makeup.

Mom and Bayleigh walk out first. The music plays and our guests turn to watch them.

I'm so nervous and excited I can barely stand it. Then, before I know it, Dad is at the door, his arm extended. "Hi, sweetheart. You ready to get married?"

I swallow. I nod. I reach for his arm.

When I step out into the still crisp night air, everyone stands in their chairs. They all turn to watch me. But all I see is Park.

He's in a suit so dark he seems to blend into the night sky. But the smile on his face is my North Star, my passage home.

I grip my dad's arm tightly as I walk up the aisle. With every step closer I get to Park, my nerves relax a bit. My heartbeat slows. I am right where I'm meant to be.

Dad stops. Park holds out his hand to shake, but

Dad leans forward and wraps him in a hug. "You take care of my baby girl," he says.

"Yes, sir," Park says.

Then my fiancé takes my hands in his. We face each other under the starlight and the twinkle lights and the heavens. The pastor says a prayer over us, and then we recite our vows.

I hear the words I always knew I'd hear, but somehow they feel new and different. Purposeful.

"You may now kiss your bride."

Park takes my face in his hands and we kiss, the softest, sweetest kiss of our lives. Fireworks burst in the sky, lighting up the stars with white and blue. It is officially a brand new year. A brand new life.

A brand new me.

Mrs. Nolan Park.

TWENTY
PARK

The whole ceremony felt like it was just a few seconds. Before I know it, I'm married. Fireworks burst over the river and people clap and the pastor congratulates us. Now it's time to party.

"Don't let me fall," Becca says as we face our family and friends and start walking down the aisle. She's been practicing walking in her heels all week, so I know she's nervous about it.

"As you wish," I say softly. Then I lean over and swoop her off her feet, cradling her in my arms.

The audience freaking loves it. Becca squeals in surprise, then wraps her arm around my neck and I carry her all the way back down the aisle. The reception is being held in the grassy meadow between two of the treehouses. With the trees and branches all wrapped in clear lights, it's a sight to behold. We sit on decorated tables under the stars and eat Texas' best BBQ.

Jace found a local band and hired them to play during the reception. So we have great food, live entertainment, and our best friends all here to party with us.

Yet all I need is her.

Becca and I sit at the head table with Jace and Bayleigh next to us. The photographer snaps photos and everyone comes up to see us and tell us how great we look. It's all a bit surreal. Even though I'm having fun, I can't wait until the night is over and everyone leaves so we can go up to our tree house and just be together as husband and wife. As soulmates.

The lights dim and the music starts playing our song. I stand up and hold out my hand to her. "Can I have this dance?"

She takes my hand and we walk out onto the wooden dancefloor that's been set up just for tonight. She wraps her arms around my neck and I hold onto her while we sway to the music. I had never heard of this song when Becca first listened to it back when we were dating. She said it was from one of her mom's favorite bands. Now it's our song. *As Long as You Love Me* by the Backstreet Boys, an old boyband from the 90's.

"This is the perfect night," I say.

Her eyes are bright and sparkly and her cheeks

are a bit flushed from the excitement of the night. "Who says you can't plan the perfect wedding in three months?"

"Maybe most people can't, but we can because we're awesome." I kiss her while we slow dance.

She peers up at me while we sway and make our way around the dance floor. Other couples join us. Her parents, Jace and Bayleigh, and even her grandparents all share this dance around us to our favorite song.

"I can't wait to start our family," Becca says.

I know she wants kids. I want kids, too. But there's no need to rush anything.

"Me too," I say, reaching up and running my hand across her cheek. "But we're already a family. You and me. Anything else is just a bonus."

ALSO BY AMY SPARLING

The Love on the Track Series

Liam Mosely is trouble. But he's also super hot.

Something tells Bella this summer won't go according to plan.

Click here to get the first book FREE!

The Team Loco Series

Three famous dirt bike racers and the girls who win their heart. A sweet YA romance series.

Click here to get the first book FREE!

ABOUT THE AUTHOR

Amy Sparling is the bestselling author of books for teens and the teens at heart. She lives on the coast of Texas with her family, her spoiled rotten pets, and a huge pile of books. She graduated with a degree in English and has worked at a bookstore, coffee shop, and a fashion boutique. Her fashion skills aren't the best, but luckily she turned her love of coffee and books into a writing career that means she can work in her pajamas. Her favorite things are coffee, book boyfriends, and Netflix binges.

She's always loved reading books from R. L. Stine's Fear Street series, to The Baby Sitter's Club series by Ann, Martin, and of course, Twilight. She started writing her own books in 2010 and now publishes several books a year. Amy loves getting messages from her readers and responds to every single one! Connect with her on one of the links below.

www.AmySparling.com

facebook.com/authoramysparling

bookbub.com/profile/amy-sparling

goodreads.com/Amy_Sparling